Six of Cups

A Circle of Stories

Erika B. Makino

⊕ EARTH BOOKS

Redwood Valley, California

Six Of Cups

Copyright © 1992 by Erika B. Makino
All rights reserved

Cover photo by Yoshi Makino

Printed in the U.S.A.
ISBN 0-929151-05-4
Library of Congress Catalog Number 92-70849

Individual copies may be ordered directly from Earth Books. Send a check or money order for $8.50 plus $1.50 for mailing. For terms on volume quantities, please contact the publisher:
Earth Books
P.O. Box 740
Redwood Valley, CA 95470

"The Broken Cup," "The Thief," and "The Blockade" were published in vols. 2, 4, and 5 of *Word Weavers, An Anthology of Prose and Poetry* by Regional Writers of The Mendocino College Community. "The Vegetable Patch" appeared in *Mayacamas Journal*, Lake County Writers' Guild, 1981. "Tuong Tu" was published in the original German version in *Annabelle*, Zurich 1964, no. 357.

Permission to use portions of the journal by Lani Ulm was kindly given by her sons.

Table of Contents

Preface 5

Finding a Voice 7
in the midst of an exam

Couple in a Tea Room 21
the old and the new world meet over a sugar cube

Tuong Tu 25
unfulfilled love between East and West

Hans-Peter 35
notes about a retarded boy

Alice 39
an epileptic child in her classroom

Vegetable Patch 41
a former boyfriend returns

The Broken Cup 47
at a ski resort

The Thief 55
a train ride in Columbia

The Press Release 57
three chilren read the news

The Visitor 61
a love story between two women

The Vigil 73
a marriage

The Blockade   85
an anti-nuclear demonstration

Painting My Brother's Face   95
an art class and the memory it awakens

A Study in Light and Shadow   99
art as a way to heal

A Tour through an Exhibit   103
transcription of a tape

The Bus Ticket   117
in a workshop for the mentally disabled

Raymond   123
who dislikes suspenders

Barry   131
who likes boys

Gerald   143
who loves his cat

Finding a Home   151
a wait at the airport

Preface

I HAD ALMOST FINISHED these stories and needed a title for my book. My friend Barbara and I were sitting on the floor in my mother's empty apartment in Switzerland. As Barbara read the Tarot to me, I was attracted to the Six of Cups. She told me that traditionally this card means "things of the past bringing pleasure in the present." I liked that. Cups hold water, the symbol of the unconscious, of feelings, emotions. The motif of cups appears several times in my book, and not merely by coincidence. Suddenly I knew that I had found the title.

These stories have been written over a span of forty years. But during the two decades when my children were growing up, I did not write. It is not unusual for a mother to give up her favorite activity.

All my stories are taken from my life. What is most true in them are my feelings, not always the facts. Just as the drawings I've included are so sketchy that even my models cannot recognize themselves, my characters are also incomplete.

In order to ease my readers from one story to the next and to create a connected, chronological tale, I have included short transitional sections which are indented to indicate shifts in perspective.

I write because I'm curious about life. I never know where my stories are going to take me, what new insights will come, what healing they will provide.

My own native language is a Swiss German dialect that is not a written language. While writing this book my thoughts and images refused to take form smoothly in ordinary English even though I immigrated to the U.S. thirty years ago. I didn't want to write in German because I no longer feel comfortable with it, and besides, I want my American friends to be able to read my stories.

Those friends who have read them have corrected the most jarring of my mistakes and patched up my hybrid German-English style without changing the faithful expression of my immigrant's heart.

My warmest thanks go to all my supportive and helpful friends; Riki, Charlotte, Werner, Henry, Ann, Jean, Annette, Carolyn, Sunlight, Jo-ann, Jan, Barbara, Charity, Lucia, Elin, Charlene, Bob, Edith, Irene, Nancy, Pat and to my daughters Annette, Yoshi and Yuri.

Erika B. Makino
Redwood Valley, California

Finding a Voice

I DIDN'T KNOW if I was I going to die or lose my mind. I was 23 years old. Something strange happened one evening as I was studying for my degree. I was reading a 19th century novel. All of a sudden I heard the writer's voice so clearly it seemed real. I felt he had come alive and his presence invaded my room. I was frightened and closed my book. For weeks I had struggled for clarity and now had it come to engulf me?

I want to look back and remember the woman I was then. I'll call her Esther because there is not much resemblance between her and me. Now I can give her the support she needed so badly then.

Esther was sitting in the library of the university. She was covering her notepaper with leaves and tendrils that curled around the words she had written. Her thoughts and daydreams were more interesting than the books she had spread over the table.

Most of the other students had left a long time ago. The room was old. It had a stucco ceiling and dark corners. The heavy volumes on the shelves were oppressive. The silence around her seemed to become deeper and more commanding. She was searching desperately for a meaning behind the multitude of facts she had to learn. She knew the meaning was there. Esther closed her books and put them in a neat pile.

It was drizzly outside. Where should she go? There was the squeal of a bicycle brake behind her. The cyclist hopped off onto the sidewalk. A face smiled broadly at her.

Hans leaned his bicycle against a tree and locked it deftly. Both of them liked the old part of the town. They walked through the crooked alleys lined with narrow houses.

She threw one quick glance toward the cathedral. It was warm, unassuming, its reddish color enticing. As always, she felt a hundred faces were turned toward her. Why is it that old buildings seem to have eyes looking at you? She wondered, but did not say it aloud; she didn't want to appear strange. Is it because all those hundreds of workers who built it hid a part of their soul in the stones, in the adornments?

They crossed the square with its cobblestones and walked along the side of the cathedral. She stopped in front of her favorite portal. Scenes from the Last Judgment were carved into the stone. People were climbing out of their graves and putting on clothes.

"See that guy over there," she pointed to a part of the frieze, "he has been trying to put his other sock on for the last 600 years. I feel sorry for him, he has such a weak body."

"Yeah, and a cold butt, too," Hans added.

They strolled under the bare chestnut trees, the gravel grating under their feet. Then the view opened up. Two hundred feet below, the Rhine was streaming by. Not majestic as usual; today it was a brownish green, morose and in a hurry. Across, on the other shore, the old houses shivered in the gray weather. The bridges below were swarming with cars, bicycles and pedestrians.

She looked reluctantly at the wet benches and the dead leaves that stuck to them. Hans took off his raincoat, folded it and put it on one of the benches. They sat down, and he put an arm around her and kissed her cheek. She hardly noticed, because a new and exciting thought had suddenly crossed her mind.

"I think my linguistics department could use some help

from you physicists."

"What?" he said, startled, and let go of her.

"See, I'm studying these complicated rules of the changes in the sound system of our language which happened over the centuries. It would be much easier for me to understand all this if I could see with my eyes how the patterns of the sound waves change. I once saw the tip of a pendulum move through sand and the pattern looked like this." She tried to draw a series of ellipses in the gravel with her shoe.

"I know what you mean," he replied, jumped up, cleared the gravel away with his hand, picked up a stick and drew the pattern in the dirt just the way she had visualized it.

She nodded, excited, "That's right... Do you think it's possible to photograph the loops and circles that the sound waves make?"

"Sure. But I still don't understand why you want to bring sound and visual patterns together."

"Why? Because they *are* together. The beauty of all this is..." Her voice trailed off. There were no words for what she saw in her mind; the world and all the creatures on it becoming one connected whole; the senses all in harmony; feelings, images, colors, sounds, smells all merging into one experience, and the universe unfolding as a translucent, joyful entity.

"What are you staring at?" Hans interrupted her.

"Oh, I was just imagining something."

She got up. She felt chilled and it was getting dark.

"What are you doing tonight?" he asked.

"What a question! I have some more tests tomorrow."

"You study too much; you are obsessed. Let's go to my apartment."

The times when they made love seemed years ago to her. Now her body felt so vulnerable that the thought of being touched sexually was unbearable. Inside her there was a tiny person swathed in a golden light who was crying and wanting desperately to get out.

"No, I'd rather not; no, not today," she said in a tense voice. "Let's move on. I'm cold."

He picked up his raincoat and put it around both of them. Walking was awkward. Without saying much they reached a busy square. She slipped from under the coat.

"There, I see the Eleven coming. I have to run, I'll call you." She squeezed his arm, dashed across the square and jumped on to the streetcar.

The next morning she rode to the university but did not attend class. Instead, she went to the cafeteria and sat down near a window. She gazed out into the garden. The plants looked faded as if life had withdrawn from them. The trees and the bushes were rigid and flat as on a postcard. She felt like crying; crying about herself and about the little person inside her. Now that person was curled up like a baby, still bathed in a little bit of golden light. Why did she have to protect that being and stand up for her? Why did she want a voice now?

Her friend Al joined her at the table.

"I don't want to take this examination," she complained. "I don't want to cram anymore. I hate this whole place and I'm scared!" It came out loud and desperate.

Al put his cup down with a clatter. A couple of students at the next table looked at her.

"That's foolish, you have to take it. What's wrong with you, why are you so upset?" He sounded annoyed, even aggressive.

"I can't explain. I feel trapped, not in control, and besides I have all these stupid tests."

"Oh well, we all go through phases of this sort. When does

your next test begin?"

"In about half an hour. I better go. It's over in the English seminar building."

"Don't worry, Jack will make it easy. Good luck."

She walked across town and arrived at the English Department. She climbed the spiral staircase. The old wood cracked under her feet. In Jack Morgan's office where the examination was taking place, she sensed an unexpected mellow atmosphere. Only one other student was taking the test, a studious and intellectual young woman. Professor Morgan placed them at a long table. Its top was covered with the carved initials of generations of students. Esther faced the window. She could not see the river, but there was a gray luminous light outside.

The professor—everyone just called him Jack—walked busily in and out of the room. He was in his 60's, had thin gray hair and blazing eyes in a baby face. She was attracted both to his wide learning and to his benevolence, and she did not mind that he was hiding his real being under a taciturn and inexpressive façade.

Each time he passed through the doorway he stooped a little. He was American and often she wondered why he had come to this place where everything must seem so small to him. He had brought a coffee pot and now he was carrying cups, cream and sugar. There was something caring about his ways. It was as though his body emitted a cloud of tiny particles that softened the room and made it glimmer with orange and gray tones. He filled a coffee cup and put it at Esther's side then moved it carefully in front of her so it would not be in her way when writing.

When she had finished her composition, she went out to the terrace and put her hands on the rough stone of the banister. Black moss grew in its crevices. She leaned over the railing and gazed into the swiftly moving water far below until she felt she was floating and everything was moving with her.

Someone called her name. It was the other student telling her that it was her turn for the oral test.

She came back into the office and felt immediately that Jack had read her paper. He looked at her searchingly as though he wanted to find out how those thoughts on the paper fit this person in front of him.

A committee member had placed himself in a corner where he seemed to fade away.

She tried hard to concentrate on Prof. Morgan's questions. She felt a tension that became gradually worse. Her answers came out short, her voice sounded compressed and abrupt. It seemed to her she knew hardly anything, and what she knew she could not formulate clearly. Words and facts were drifting away. Instead a different plane unfolded invitingly before her. The solidity of the plaster walls, the sturdiness of the book cases became questionable. The physical environment was thinning and at any moment could turn into see-through drapes and let her look into the framework of personalities, into people's emotions, into the silent stretching, bending and curling of every living thing. Every shape, every movement was ready to reveal its purpose and meaning to her. The world of everyday life was receding; she was alone, cut off and there was nobody willing to follow her into the mysterious surrounding.

When she left, she knew she had done poorly. She walked through the streets aimlessly until she felt tired and decided to go home. As soon as she was in the streetcar, the familiar smell of brass and wood closed in on her. She sat down, reluctantly breathing the air that was saturated with stale smoke and the steam of moist clothes. More people got on at the next stop. The conductor squeezed his way through with his "Tickets, please!" The dim lights made everyone's face look vague and blotchy.

The streetcar had left the city behind. Esther looked out of the window into the darkness, not thinking about anything in particular while inside her mind ideas tried to become form. They wove in and out, haunting her without becoming conscious. It was like sitting in a theater and hearing the sounds from behind the closed curtain: the shuffling of feet, the moving of heavy objects, running steps.

At each curve of the tracks the wheels of the streetcar screeched. The slamming of doors accompanied the stops. She let her body go limp and let it be thrust forward or pushed back into the seat. Signs in white enamel plates with bold black letters demanded to be read: "Do not lean out of the window! Do not throw the tickets on the floor!" The trip seemed endless.

She looked around. The few passengers left were listless and uncommunicative. Even the lights had become tired, and darkness grew from under the seats. She wondered what would happen if the streetcar suddenly stopped and the passengers were let out at some place where nobody was living. At once they would break their masks, they would become alert, would have to acknowledge each other, relate, be human. Then she imagined they would all die in a crash and transform into weightless bodies. They would wander together through wondrous gates, over long roads and mountain peaks to other brilliant worlds.

"Holy Grove!" the conductor called. "Holy Grove!" as though he knew she was daydreaming and about to miss her stop.

She stepped out of the smoky car into the brisk country air. The streetcar rattled away and disappeared behind the trees. The sky had cleared up partially and the stars of the Big Dipper were flickering. She saw her parents' house, and the kitchen and hall lights glimmered invitingly.

That evening she meant to go through a stack of her notes, but she realized she would be unable to retain the facts and the dates. Tomorrow was her last examination, an oral test about German literature. She picked up a book; it was by Gottfried Keller. She began to read, listening carefully to his style. She felt his warmth, his sadness. Suddenly she could hear his voice; it became clearer and clearer as though the author were in her room near her, sitting in a chair and talking to her. She was scared and slammed the book closed. Everything was normal again. What was going on? She went to bed, not to sleep but to think. What's happening to me, she thought, why am I different? I want to examine carefully how other people think, especially my teachers. I'll stop hating and fighting it for a moment and really look at it.

She visualized how other people came to their conclusions. She saw a straight line that moved forward step by step. Her professors used that process. With some of her women friends it was different. In their conversations they started out with a feeling, then explored around it, expanding from there in all directions. In her mind she was seeing the academic thinking process as a lighted narrow band proceeding through the darkness. Her own way of thinking appeared as a brilliant point that threw its rays out like a star. She saw the line moving steadily ahead. Suddenly Esther lost control of her images. They became independent and began to move without her orders. She was amazed to see the white line bending and gradually spiraling around the point. First it spiraled slowly then faster and faster. The image became a dangerous whirlpool. It was frightening. She was losing herself, she was drowning somewhere into nothingness. She cried, "Oh my God, help!" At once the spiral merged with the center and she felt a blow near her solar plexus. Its impact, like an orgasm, shot through her whole body, to the tips of her fingers, to her toes. Then there was a deep quiet and peace. It was like being reborn. She fell asleep.

The next morning, light streamed into her room. She felt a fresh power inside her. She dressed quickly to be in time for her last test. The people in the street car were warm and friendly. She felt closeness and love for them.

She was confident and alert when she entered the examination. Her answers were prompt. She wished the questions presented more of a challenge. The last question was supposed to be hard. Professor Black asked her about Gottfried Keller. She felt she had met him last night in person. It was easy to answer all the questions.

She spent the next hours in the library. Then Al approached and whispered to her that the results of the examination were out and that she had failed. She managed a laugh. Only rarely did students fail. It was Jack who had failed her. Why Jack? She knew she couldn't have done so poorly. He wants me out of the university, she thought. But why? What does he want me to do or to become? She was puzzled.

She left the library to go to the registrar's office. On the way she met Professor Morgan. He beckoned her to a bench where they both sat down.

"What are your plans for the future?" he asked, looking inquiringly at her.

"I don't know," she said, laughing a little.

"Do you know the result of the examination?"

"Yes, I know, I failed," she said lightly.

"So, what are you going to do now?" he sounded stern.

She shrugged her shoulders. "I would prefer to do nothing at all."

"That's not much," he said gruffly and got up abruptly.

She had seconds to make a decision. Either to accept the fact that she was seen as dumb, and conform to that view, or else challenge it. She had the habit of not speaking up. Too many times she was not heard, either by her own family or later by her classmates. The way she put things did not make sense to the others no matter how strongly she felt about an issue. There was a world out there that was "theirs," a world that was not interested in hers.

But today there was a power on her side which changed the balance in her favor. Professor Morgan had turned and was walking away. She got up, caught up with him and said, "Excuse me."

He stopped immediately. "I would like to explain something," she said, searching frantically for words.

"It is true that I did not always pay attention in your class, but it was not because I was not interested. I was trying to find out in my mind..." Professor Morgan was looking intensely at her. "I was thinking," she continued, "how you could see everything in a different way. I mean—for instance—I could express any form..." She looked around for some object, saw a column and said, "I could express this form in words; not what I imagine or fantasize, but what's really in it."

At that moment Professor Morgan took a step sideways, or it was rather a leap to the left.

"For *you* it is like that, not for me," he said under his breath.

"Is that all absurd?"

"I can't say anything else."

"I can't explain it very well right now, but I could write it down."

"You can write me a letter."

He looked again sharply at her, mumbled a good-bye and walked away.

He hadn't understood her, but there was hope. There was an opening, a possibility to communicate. She would write a long letter to him and explain her ideas carefully.

It was spring semester break and no classes for two weeks. She tried to write to Jack but soon realized that her thoughts did not fit into even a long letter. There was just too much to say. How about writing a story? Actually she didn't want to become a writer because what she longed to express was exact, it was more like science and not at all like fiction.

She cleaned up her desk and got some paper out. She sat there for hours, covering pages with doodles and here and there a line of words. This is the real test, she thought, everything before this was nothing. Fear crawled up her back. But the feeling was different. This time the test was fair and she had a chance of winning.

Finally it dawned on her that she could not build a story with shapes, patterns and feelings. She needed human beings to write about. She scanned her friends and acquaintances in her mind. Suddenly it was perfectly clear that she had to write about Murray and Kathleen, two friends she had made in London, an American man and an English woman, representatives of the old and the new world.

Writing the story was a struggle which lasted for days. It was short but compact. She entitled it, "Couple in the Tea Room." She got out her father's old typewriter to type it. Her heart was beating fast. She would not have been surprised if the machine had refused to print her words. They looked blunt and naked on the page. Could she dare to show this to anybody?

She wrote Professor Morgan's address on an envelope. There was something strangely familiar and emotional about his name. She walked to the mailbox, not because she really wanted to, but rather because some force drove her there in spite of her fear. She opened the lid slowly and dropped the letter in. It fell into the dark. What have I done? she wondered.

I want to end Esther's story here. But I have to add that I know for sure Jack was touched by the first attempt of literary work by one of his students even though he never said a word about her short story. That young person craved his support, yearned for his wisdom to show her the way through life. But he couldn't give it.

I remember the semester had come to a close. I needed Professor Morgan's signature on a form. I climbed the winding staircase to his office for the last time, knocked at the door. He was sitting at his desk. When he saw me, he looked startled, then composed himself quickly. He got up.

"What can I do for you?"

"Could you please sign this paper?"

He looked at it for a long time. It took so long he could have memorized it. Finally he signed it.

He asked me what my plans were for the future. I told him that I was going to work in an office. He said something about other authors who had to hold a job, too, to make a living and he gave the names of some of the novelists I had studied.

Then he added, "Think about writing something longer." He stretched out his hand, shook mine and said softly goodbye. He wished me all the best, then turned around quickly.

I hurried downstairs, my footsteps echoing through the building. I stepped out into the street and felt that Jack was at the window, his glance following me. I didn't turn around. I hurt badly inside.

> Only much later did I understand that Jack failed me because he wanted me to be out in real life and write instead of spending years at the university to pursue a scholarly career.
>
> I'm going to share the story I wrote for Jack. Even today after so many years I'm reluctant to let people read it. This short account is like a new born baby you hesitate to let strangers hold. The story is about a man

and a woman but it's not about two people but about three. I'm in it also, invisible, climbing into Kathleen's then Murray's body, lending them my sentience.

Couple in a Tea Room

HE ENTERED FIRST. He was tall and handsome. His forehead was high and curved outward at the sides as though he was striving for something far away. His lips were of such a perfect shape, that you were afraid he could never find the goodness he needed. Between mouth and forehead there was a strange emptiness.

She followed him. Her feet were turned outward, and she held her light body rigidly tilted forward. She seemed to be blown rather than walking, as if lacking human will to give her direction. They sat down across from each other.

With their bodies relaxed and the quietness between them, feelings and images rose in the man and in the woman. When he looked at her finally, she seemed to be a stranger. He remembered whenever he wanted to kiss her, she drew her head in and then turned it sideways with closed eyes. Sometimes she hinted to him that he should marry her, then her voice became indistinct. It was just as blurry when she told him about the illness of her relative. He felt she was without a center, her consciousness a wheel without its hub with no knowledge of good and bad. She could talk all right about life's dramas but she could not really experience them. He saw her wide lower jaw, her flat face, her eyes that saw everything without perspective. Now he smelled her perfume, and something uncanny wanted to suck him in and down. He turned away and thought about the distant continent where he came from, the heat, the brilliance of the light, the ranch.

She rested her eyes on him while he reached for a newspaper. His movements started at his shoulders and went too far. There was something useless about them. She was thinking of his jokes that never reached her, and how she laughed out of politeness. Still sometimes when she heard him coming into her apartment, her heart raced as if an infinite power was coming to annihilate her. It was like his palms that were too large, full of an inexpressible promise. But when he pulled her against him, she felt that he didn't want to possess her, he was trying in vain to heal a deep hurt. Then suddenly he let go of her.

He doesn't keep any appointment, she thought; he comes to me whenever he pleases, he lets himself drop into an armchair and falls asleep or he reads a travel book in front of my fireplace, then leaves.

He threw a piece of sugar into his tea glass. A column of tiny bubbles rose quickly to the surface. He observed how the liquid ate a hole into the cube and broke it apart. She saw the edges decaying and the grains purling down. He took the spoon and mashed the sugar into small pieces.

"I think I won't go with you next weekend," she said abruptly. He looked up in surprise. Then he would have to prepare his meals himself, he thought; without her company there would be too much of himself. He changed the topic. She had a liking for comical situations and human weaknesses, although she spoke with grace and without mockery. He listened to her supple voice that seemed to receive and hold gently to everything imperfect, a voice that wanted to give and help. Sometimes she talked with her hands, while holding her arms close to her body and spreading her fingers like leaves opening up. As she lifted her eyebrows an exquisite expression of enchantment slid over her face.

Later, when they left, he put his arm around her shoulders and leaned on her.

> That summer I wrote another story. I sent it to Jack though I feared he would not respond. He didn't.
> The story was about a Vietnamese painter I had met in Paris two years before. I had kept some of his letters,

and when I read through them once more, the time we had spent together became vivid again. Like Jack he was a kind of mentor who led me for a short distance on my way through life.

Tuong Tu

"I AM GOING TO SHOW YOU how we prepare rice in Indochina. Watch me and when you go back to your country you can cook it in the same way and then you will perhaps remember me." His smile enveloped the pain of our parting.

He took two handfuls of grain from a hemp sack and sprinkled it into a saucepan, which he filled several times with water to wash the rice. Then he refilled the pan, dipped his finger into it and said:

"Look, there are two parts rice and one part water."

He lit a match, bent down and held it to the kerosene stove that was on the floor. Flames burst out, and he put the rice on to boil.

The buzzing noise of Paris entered through the open window. The smoky air that streamed in was mingled with the mellow smell of chestnut trees.

He pulled the table nearer to the couch and sat down. He took packages of oysters, meat and vegetables from a basket.

I loved to watch him because he moved with sureness and precision, and there seemed to be a close relationship between him and the objects he touched.

"Come, sit nearer to me," he said. "Can you remember when we met for the first time? Why did you choose me to ask for that address...? When we had to cross a street, I looked at you and then you took my hand. Suddenly an emotion overwhelmed me. Oh, I cannot express what I felt at that moment." He became silent and our first meeting was again present to us.

I remembered how I had been standing there, shy and self-conscious, looking for someone whom I might ask. But all those faces passing by were so busy thinking about things that seemed to lie far ahead of them. When he came along, there was calmness about him. I spoke to him and forgot at once that he was a stranger and that he belonged to another race.

He started to prepare the vegetables.

"No, don't help me. I want to do everything myself because it is our last meal together."

We were in a small room with a floor made of red stone tiles. Maps from Europe and Asia covered the shabby walls. There was an easel near the window holding one of his paintings, one he had entitled "La Vendeuse de Jouets." It was done on silk with light pastel colors and a few contrasting dark shades. The woman in the picture was smiling. Her hands were holding two ends of a rod from which toys were hanging. Children stretched out their arms to reach them. There was an illusion of depth in the picture but no focal point. It was filled with a friendly dreaminess, and when I looked at it for a long time, it seemed to lure me away into a world of forgetting, of mysterious floating, and of unknown delight.

I looked at my friend. He was quietly busy cutting an onion into neat tiny cubes. I thought, "Even this he can do better than I."

There was something like envy inside me which kept me from loving him completely. I realized that his character was already formed, whereas I still lived in a world of hazy outlines. He was not only older and more mature than I, but besides this, his Oriental mind seemed to be aware of something of great consequence that was still hidden to me. His mere presence made me conscious of it and filled me with expectation. One day that secret would be open to me, too. In the meantime I would try to understand him more and more.

"Do you know," I said, "the first time I really felt happy with you was the moment when I entered your room and discovered this print by Paul Klee above your couch? There was something we both liked, something common I could grasp. It occurred to me that the point, the truth Klee was referring to, does not lie in the limited range of the Western tradition, but it must exist somewhere outside where we both have equal access."

"Yes, I remember," he smiled, "and then we looked through a volume of reproductions of Klee's paintings and you took more interest in the book than in me."

He had finished peeling and cutting and went to the basin to wash his hands. He looked in the mirror.

"Do you think that I look tired? The climate in this city is not healthy."

I was already used to the strange variability of his features. He never looked quite the same as before and seemed to be adapting his physical appearance to laws unknown to me.

"Come here," he said. I went over to him. He put his arms round my neck.

"Tell me once more the impression you get from the forms of my lips, from my flat nose, from my Oriental eyes."

"I have told you before."

"All right, then tell me just once more what impression you get from the whole of my face."

I mused, then I ventured to say:

"It reminds me of a very young plant that has not yet developed branches or anything." We laughed.

"Try once more."

"Well, your face is flat, it stretches to both sides, like a long wall. It is endless. Endless things are cold. We white people seem to have a center behind our faces, from which heat comes."

He became thoughtful and let me go. After a while he replied:

"In twenty years you will look very different, but I won't

have changed so much. You Caucasians have more characteristic features than we, but age marks you more, too. I always get the impression that you destroy yourselves."

"We must look ugly to you," I said.

"The first days after my arrival in Europe it was very unpleasant to see all those pink faces around me, with long noses and bulging eyes. But now I am accustomed to it."

I looked in the mirror and said, "Sometimes I see myself with your eyes, then I feel plump and awkward."

"No, you are all right."

I was not convinced. And I had other doubts as to my person and my attitudes. Compared to his life, whole stretches of mine looked empty. I had wasted them either by regretting things that had happened or by hoping for others to come. He was different. Each moment seemed to bring to him the experience of perfection and fullness. Life was not a drama to him. It was more like a continual pattern. From each section he expected completion, and when he judged human beings, he did not take into account their past nor the goals they were striving for. I was aware that his attitude aimed at a perfection of one's being to an extent I had not dreamed of until now.

The sounds of a radio entered the room from somewhere in the building. The voice of a woman sang, "...que mon coeur se brise...." She affected a kind of passion that was far from real.

He was annoyed and said, "Why does she sing in that way? I don't like the French, they are so crude in their feelings. They are good in debating and thinking, but I don't like them... and they are not clean. The women in my country are much more sensitive than you, but they do not have your education."

He stepped to the easel and examined his painting.

"Soon I want to exhibit my paintings again. Not because I am ambitious for material rewards. But I want to make my pictures known, and I believe I have that right. At each one of my exhibitions I sensed that my work had created a community on a higher level."

I remembered when I had entered the art gallery for the first time to see his paintings, and I remembered how they had overwhelmed me, surpassing all my expectations. I could see, of course, that it was his hands that had painted the pictures, but what he had expressed was not his personality. Something which existed outside his being had passed through him and he had caught it and cast it on the canvas. But it had left him empty. In the presence of his paintings he himself had seemed meaningless to me, and I had thought then that I could leave him for good.

I had nearly forgotten his bodily presence, and when he moved and came to me, I hurried to collect my thoughts. He sat at my side on the couch and began, "You accompany me through a fraction of my life and I discover in you rare qualities."

I was startled each time he made this grammatical mistake and used the present instead of the past, but the correct tense seemed to contradict his feelings. Before my inner eyes he appeared with time streaming by always at the same speed.

His person seemed strangely void of a beginning and an end, and he seemed to cling to another being that was bigger than himself—a mysterious, transcendent force. For him each point of time was open to eternity. He recalled the most significant moments and listened to them as he would listen to an echo. Often I was not able to grasp the slight differences in the meaning of his words, but his mere presence was full of suspense: he seemed to possess the key that would open another life for me.

He spoke again, "Your capacity to understand me is comforting, and it gives me the strength to put my ideas into reality. You may believe it or not, but I had to tell you because your fingers touched strings and a tune awoke within me whose title is 'You and I.' And if your fingers never play again, this music has vibrated into the air that is surrounding us. I am now tired of what I have seen and I can close my eyes and listen to it. Soon you are going to another country, but perhaps you will come back and then everything that links us will be pure and perfect."

I loved his words but my mind was doubtful.

"Come," he said, "let's rest until dinner is ready and I will tell you a legend. But in order to be able to understand it, you must know that the people of my country believe that for every human being there has been a counterpart since all eternity, and that those pairs will meet on this earth."

He took a plate, put it on his knees, pointed to its edge and said, "You were born here, and there is where I was born." He pointed to the other edge. Then he drew his index fingers to the middle of the plate.

"Here we met. Maybe we are destined for each other."

He got up and turned down the flame under the rice. The grains had swollen and the water had evaporated. He put the lid on. Some vapor still found its way out. He took a piece of paper, tucked it under the lid and covered the pan tight. Then he stretched himself beside me.

"Let me think a moment," he said.

My eyes wandered along his body, which seemed to belong to a young boy. I saw the slight irregular proportions of his frame. His narrow chest between his strong arms made me feel uneasy. His neck was muscular and, to me, the only Caucasian thing about him. There was a hold on life in it, and it was good. In his face there was the contrast between his youthful mouth and his much older-looking forehead.

He bent over me and began to speak. He talked low, with

passion, and his voice vibrated with the sound of a sad child. I could not resist and completely forgot reality.

"Once upon a time there was a Chinese official who had a beautiful daughter. Like all the young girls of her class she was not allowed to see anyone and lived secluded in the high tower of her father's palace. Often she looked down to the river where a fisherman with his boat used to pass. She could not see him well but she could hear him singing. His voice was beautiful; his song was sad. One morning he did not appear. For several days she waited in vain. She fell ill. Only when the song reached her room again did she recover. The mandarin learned the cause of his daughter's illness and asked the fisherman to visit her. As soon as she saw him something was finished inside her. She did not want to hear his voice anymore. The meeting was fatal to the fisherman: he was seized by the sickness Tuong Tu, the suffering from hopeless love. He wasted away and died.
"Many years later his family found a transparent stone in his tomb. The mandarin saw it, bought it and had a teacup made from it. Each time someone poured tea into it, a fisherman in his boat appeared and circled the cup. The daughter of the mandarin heard of the miracle and wanted to see it herself. She poured some tea into the cup: the image of the fisherman appeared. She remembered and wept. A tear fell on the cup which melted and disappeared."

For a while we did not talk. I was moved by the story and felt tears in my eyes. The humming sound of the city came from the window. The flames on the stove flickered when a draft swept through the room.
I looked at my friend. He had closed his eyes, and his thick black hair hung down over his forehead. Suddenly I noticed that his skin had stretched tight over his face and that his fea-

tures had become completely even and beautiful. Age and individuality had vanished, and it was as though he had gone away into a remote world and had left me behind with a multiplied consciousness of myself.

"I am leaving tonight," I thought, "but it does not make much difference because what I love is eluding me, or I'm not ready for it." I felt restless and thought sadly how far away I was from the serenity that radiated from his face.

After a while he opened his eyes and said, "I think the rice must be ready by now." He got up, lifted the saucepan from the fire and quickly prepared the other food. When we sat down at the table, he grabbed a fork while I picked up a pair of chopsticks and we ate in silence.

> I saw my Vietnamese friend a few more times. But later, when I lived in the United States, I stopped writing to him. I was embarrassed. What would he think of me if I told him that I had chosen to stay in the country that was killing his people and destroying his homeland? Years later, when I returned to Europe, I searched for him.
>
> "He is dead," a friend said. "He died of tuberculosis a long time ago." I was shocked. Where was I when he died? Did I ever think of him when he was ill? Why did he have to die so young? Was it because we Westerners did not understand and accept him and his people?
>
> I remembered the story of the fisherman. Suddenly it occurred to me that my friend had wasted away exactly like the man in the folk tale. I felt my heart being squeezed. I was sad for a long time
>
> I felt homeless after I left the University. I was confused and lonely. When my office job was over, I tried teaching. Soon I realized that I could not teach thirty children simultaneously. Thirty pairs of eyes were looking at me but I could not see any of the children. I needed a one-to-one relationship or a group that was so small that I still could be aware of the emotions of the individual child.
>
> A challenging Special Education course seemed to be waiting just for me and I enrolled. As one of the projects

we visited regularly a class of twelve-year old retarded boys and girls. There was a boy in the class who caught my attention immediately. He was different and there was a secret about him that intrigued me.

The boy's name was Hans-Peter. He was taller than the other children and quite handsome though his face was strangely void of expression. He was not well coordinated in his movements. Besides that, I could not discover anything special about him. Still, I felt compelled to follow him with my eyes. If I did not watch him, I feared I would miss something.

At one point, the instructor wrote the names of the children on pieces of paper. We had to draw a name and write a report about that particular child. The hat with the names was passed around. I pulled out a paper, unfolded it and read "Hans-Peter." I was very happy.

After weeks of observing him I wrote the report. It was not a meaningful paper and later I threw it away. But I kept my notes. They contained observations which could not be included in an academic report.

Hans-Peter

INTELLIGENCE TEST: *He has an IQ of 72, close to the range of the other children.*

Rorschach Test: Reveals nothing unusual, but his reaction was striking. His normally placid behavior changed and he suddenly became animated and happy.

April 27. Hans-Peter came to me before class and told me that he had stepped on a snail and crushed it. It was strange how he told me. He talked in an indifferent way without any guilt or joy, in a kind of gray voice as though his feelings were diffused and he was being one with the snail, with the acting boy and with the whole scene—without any distance of objectivity.

There is not much to observe during class time. All the time he sits quietly on his bench.

Drawings: his figures are always close to each other. No arms. Their bodies are surrounded by what appears to be a watery world. He always divides the sheet into two horizontal strips. This way he can produce two drawings and gets two focal points on the same page.

Rhythm and Music class: Something odd going on here. I don't know what it is.

May 2. Hans-Peter was skipping today. His head was bent and did not lead the way for the torso. I had this flash of him being an infant. Like a baby's, Hans-Peter's body seemed to be like a big ear with the capacity to listen to the universe.

May 9. I noticed something very strange today. The teacher made him jump forward. He was afraid and did not want to do it. After a struggle with himself he did it anyway. Just before he jumped his *body became rigid. Then I sensed a strange convulsive motion in the boy and it seemed as though, within his body, a second person tried to separate from the first.*

His face is not always a blank. For less than a second I perceived something. It seemed there were two faces, or two expressions, that quickly merged and then extinguished each other, and there was the blank again. I feel the blank is like a threshold that separates two spaces. It's timeless.

May 15. I'm trying to reproduce the thoughts and feelings I had when I saw Hans-Peter in the school yard.

There is Hans-Peter and he is coming toward me. No, he is not coming but his head is bobbing up and down. A strange way to move about. He is not walking. He is Christ ascending or some other holy figure. He is coming forward. What an awkward way of rolling his feet off the ground. He will never reach me, he will never reach anybody. But he is approaching. Here he is.

Rhythm class: The children were beating the rhythm with wooden sticks. Hans-Peter beat a little too early each time. It seemed he was cutting through a living chain that was woven from one child to another, and he created something different. With each beat he was forming a dark vertical line. I know this line. It is the vertical of the cross that pierces the horizontal of the physical plane. Is it at this intersection where birth and death meet where this boy has his home?

May 28. I gave Hans-Peter the projection test once more. It's hard to describe my experience. For a moment the two of us seemed to be transported into another reality. He looked at the ink blots as if we were going to play the best game in the world. He asked joyfully, "Is this a butterfly? Is this a flower?" He became so happy to talk to his own self, that he somehow transformed the dreary room into a space that was flooded with light. His voice became like a lover's who was asking for the last time "Do you love me?" before merging with his other self.

Hans-Peter's world had touched me with magic and didn't let go of me for the next three years. I found employment in a home for retarded youngsters. Little eggshells from a previous existence were still clinging to these children and I had much to wonder about while I was with them.

One of the strangest of my pupils was Alice.

Alice

IT'S DIFFICULT TO LIKE ALICE. I see her coming into the school room. Below the shadow of her black hair her face seems to be sliding apart. She is walking as though the floor were not level; nor can she walk in a straight line. Waves appear to come from the left, crash into her and push her sideways. Big circles surround her like empty bowls she is offering us to fill with our attention and caring. They are much too large for us.

Now she tries to grab a chair but her hand stops before she has touched it. It seems she is not quite sure what is solid and what is air. I put a piece of paper and crayons on her desk. She sits down and, as always, reaches for the green and the blue. Is she compelled to paint forever the beginning of creation when the land is separated from the water? I ask her a question. Her answer is delayed. She is out of sync with our rhythm. Later I see her drawing the bird's face onto his belly.

Her voice has to force itself out of a narrow tunnel. I feel my heart closing up when she speaks because it is frightening. Her voice sounds like the wind howling through a chimney or like the voices of unborn spirits clamoring in a cave. With every word she speaks, Alice is screaming for help.

Suddenly she is falling off her chair. She has a seizure. The other children and I kneel around her. I cradle her head, the others are holding her shaking limbs. We feel sorry for her, we love her. There is a feeling of reconciliation and warmth.

I saw Alice for the last time when she walked through the hall on her mother's arm. Her movements were rigid, her shoulder when I touched it was like wood. I noticed that her mother's face was lit up as though a blissful light were falling through the opening high up in the wall.

Once I dreamt of her. She is standing on a little elevation.

Other people and I are living down below in small blue cubes near a shore. The lanes of our village are so narrow that Alice cannot enter them.

    It's time for a cup of tea. I watch the water coming to a boil. I listen to its hum. Little bubbles form here and there. Finally big ones erupt from the bottom of the pot and transform the quiet surface into a turmoil.
    I carry my cup outdoors into the sunshine together with some papers. I have to deal with something unpleasant. It's one of my stories which I have to re-read and perhaps correct. Fear settles under the skin of my cheeks and my breath is getting shallow. Still now, after so many years!

The Vegetable Patch

A COUNTRY ROAD wound around the hillside. It was a warm summer afternoon. When a car passed—which happened rarely—a cloud of dust rose, twirled and settled reluctantly. A few oak trees cast their deep black shadows over the road.

A young, slender woman was walking along, carrying a hoe in her hand. A bulging blue jeans pocket revealed an apple. She had come from the city to her parents' ranch for a visit. Today she had decided to do some weeding in their vegetable patch two miles down the road. As a child she had disliked this kind of work but now she was looking forward to it. Having all that space for herself would be good. "Nobody else, just the weeds and me," she thought, "and maybe a heron in the sky."

Just then a car came from the opposite direction, slowing down as it passed her. It turned around and stopped on the other side of the road. A man stepped out.

"Oh, it's John!"

He had been her boyfriend four years ago, before she had moved to the city. She thought, "It will be fun to talk to him, exchange experiences." How many ice-cream cones they had licked, how many movies they had seen together! Everything came back to her as she watched him walking towards her. They had swum in the river and finally, where the underbrush was thick, made love a few times. Her memory became blurry. What happened? Was it that from then on all he wanted from her was sex? Did she end the relationship? Anyhow, soon after that she moved away. Now she was curious to find out what had become of him!

He crossed the road and smiled with his slightly sheepish smile that she knew so well. It was more like an embarrassed and devious grin. She liked the expression of his eyes better with their mischievous twinkle.

"Hello, Mary," he called, "are you living here again?" He pulled her against his chest and went on, "I'm on my way to your village to do some business. You look great. Come and have a look at my car. I just bought it. It cost me a lot of money." He pulled his tie off and flung it through the open car window. "Do you like her?" he patted the roof.

Before she could answer he talked about his business and how fast he was getting ahead. She wondered which of his many interests he had pursued and asked him about his hobbies. The question embarrassed him.

"No time for stuff like that anymore," he said and with a wave of his hand he dismissed the topic.

She began talking about her life in the city and her job but he hardly listened. He only wanted to know how many boyfriends she had. She felt frustrated. "Why doesn't he hear me?" she thought.

"Where are you going?" he asked.

"To my parents' vegetable patch. Weeding."

"Oh good. I'll go with you."

"You must be kidding. What's so great about a vegetable patch? Let's have a drink together instead. I can weed tomorrow."

"No, we are going to your patch. I want to see it." She wondered, was it because she was not dressed up that he did not want to take her out, or did he not want to be seen with her for other reasons?

He asked, "What do you have in your pocket?" She pulled out the apple and handed it to him. He broke it in half, and they shared it as they had done many times before.

They walked along the road slowly. She felt that he was scrutinizing her body. She looked at him, saw his narrowed glance. Then she knew: he wanted sex.

She thought about making love for a moment: Lying down on the warm ground, watching the bugs climbing the grasses; listening to each other and communicating; touching each other's body, gently, gently; feeling and sharing the feeling; melting into each other, melting away...

But no, not with John. From the moment he had stepped from his car he had treated her like a non-person, not listening to her. She had to get out of this situation.

"How is your mother, John?"

"Okay, I guess. I don't have time to visit the old lady an awful lot."

"How is her arthritis?"

"I don't know," he said gruffly.

They left the road, followed a narrow path and a minute later they were in the vegetable patch. Mary put her hoe on the big rock which used to be her playhouse when she was a child.

She admired the chard. It was growing lusciously, its leaves juicy green and fleshy. The smell of the onions tickled her nose. Suddenly John was at her side and stuck his hand into her blouse. She thrust his hand out and stepped back.

"I'm not your girlfriend anymore. You have seen the patch, so let's go back," and she started marching toward the road.

"Just wait a moment," he said, following her and pulling her around.

"You don't have any right over me," she screamed.

"*Who* says I don't have any right over you?" He grabbed her tighter, "and since when are you so damned prudish? You didn't use to be like that."

She struggled to get away from him. His hands were like wrenches around her body. He tried to pull her jeans down over her hips, but couldn't.

"Stop it! Stop it!" she screamed.

He seemed to have six arms; whenever she freed one of

hers, he caught it again. Every fiber of his muscles was prepared to attack and defend but never to let go, never to yield. He had only one goal: to dominate, to win. But *her* body, disbelieving that she really wanted to hurt someone, did not obey her.

She aimed her fist at his nose but missed. Her blows came down weakly. She wanted to jam her knee into his groin but she could not get into the right position. He frustrated her intention to strike him by jerking her arm away more violently, and tightening his grip. His belt buckle dug a wide gash into her arm. She hardly felt it—her whole body was already burning. She noticed her struggling getting weaker and her screams louder and more desperate.

She was defending herself but she had not known until now how deep her self was. It went down and down until it reached glass—clear, cool water. Many people had come to drink from it. They were kneeling down, looking at it in wonder. They were scooping it into their hands and taking long draughts. Mary thought, they are drinking love and trust. They need it to stay human. But here was this monster who was about to soil and poison the water. She must defend it all by herself. Her anguish grew.

John's hand drove over her crotch like a scooter. "Mother, help," her lips only moved. Then loudly, "Help! Help!" Her screams pierced the air. She thought, "I'll have to kick his balls." All of a sudden she stopped struggling and said, "Okay, let's do it." A short grin went over his face. She commanded, "Open your pants, you sheephead!"

Even now he did not let go of her. He kept one hand on her forearm, his fingers like a clamp, squeezing her bones together. With the other hand he opened his belt, opened the button, pulled the zipper. It got stuck.

"Damn it!" He had to use both hands and let go of her. In a flash she was on top of the rock, the hoe raised in her hands, ready to strike.

"I'll kill you," she said in cold rage.

Suddenly everything was quiet. She felt light and strong and her body was one with the hoe. Her vision was clear as never before. She knew she could not miss that head.

He came closer. He looked up at her and immediately averted his glance.

"I guess you don't want to make love," he said lightly and began arranging his clothes. "I know other women who are not crazy like you." He turned and walked away.

She stood on the rock a while longer. Then she climbed up the hill, her hands still tightly around the hoe. Now she could see him walking along the road, then getting into the car and driving off.

She returned to the vegetable patch. Hacking furiously at the dandelions, she cursed and sobbed, "I hate you, I hate you; you are so sick, sick, sick," and the weeds flew up into the air.

> The tea in my cup is cold. My visit to the past was a long and intense one. Here in the present everything seems peaceful. The leaves of the manzanita bushes are swaying a little. I notice a spider running across the deck and disappearing in a crack. Good. It vanished like a bad memory should.

※

> I'm going to insert a story here which I wrote long after I had left my native Switzerland. I had settled in California where the emotional space between the people is friendly but cool and wide. Once I was used to it I liked it. Still, one day I felt the need to conjure up memories of a landscape where people are intricately enmeshed with each other by a long common history.

The Broken Cup

MY BOYFRIEND MARTIN and I were running a small eating place above a ski resort in Switzerland. It was a gloomy late afternoon in December. The humming and clicking of the ski-lift had stopped early that day, and the last of our customers had left. I was drying dishes and putting them back on the shelves. I remember it was so dark that we had kept the light on all day.

It had been a bad day. Martin and I had had an argument in the morning. I, irritated for some reason, had said to him, "Why don't you do the important things first, like fixing the broken lamp and the oven door, instead of puttering around in the workshop?" He got very angry because I had criticized him, and he screamed at me. He stomped through the dining room, kicked a box, lifted up a chair and slammed it on the floor. I was scared. Although he never hit me, I felt threatened. I did not know how to stop him, I just froze.

He shouted, "You are just careless, that's why all our appliances break, and then you want me to fix them." Of course, this did not make sense. Why should I have broken the old lamp and the oven door? I was simply using them. I did not say much because, if I replied, his voice would become louder, more threatening, and his arguments more irrational.

I looked out the window. The sky was a heavy gray. There was not much snow. Under the trees it had started to melt away, and the brown patches with the pine needles had grown big. I worried that soon we would not have guests anymore.

Martin calmed down, but inside my head the fight was still going on. I repeated his words, "You have broken the lamp, the oven door." Again I replied in my thoughts, "I did not do anything wrong, they just broke." It went on, like a record I could not turn off.

My mind rejected his blame, but some part of me was open and prepared to believe him. His accusations, like a hostile substance, penetrated my body, seeped deeper and deeper and slowly settled around my bones. And still the record went on, "It's all your fault!" "It's not, it just happened."

It was cool, so I put a heavy log on the fire and opened the draft on the stove pipe. Martin wandered in and out from the workshop.

I carried his coffee cup to the kitchen, washed and dried it and put it carefully in its place on the shelf. If it were not in its place, he would not try to find it. He would just stand there behind me and say impatiently, "Where is my coffee cup?" I would not have to turn around to know his stance: feet apart, arms hanging down without touching his body, hands almost in fists and his body ready to lunge forward. And he would repeat, annoyed, "Where is my coffee cup?" I would stop breathing. His aggressive mood would be pounding my back, and impending destruction would be like a black rainbow above my head. I would locate the cup somewhere and give it to him with a numb hand.

Martin had settled at a table in the dining room, reading a magazine. I was glad the counter was between us.

Since I had been living with Martin I watched every move I made, every word I said, so I would not anger him. I was nervous. The more I held back from expressing myself, the more tense I got. The tension was no longer limited to my body, it had begun to distort the space we lived in. When Martin was across from me, the room was pulled apart sideways; the walls that were to the right and the left of me bent outwards. Martin was brought closer and closer and the space between us became denser and denser.

I dropped a serving spoon. The noise scared me because I

thought Martin would scream at me again—but he didn't. When I picked it up, I saw my face in its shiny surface. My mouth was grotesquely enlarged, and my head was all flat. I turned the spoon and focused it until my head was elongated and all brain. I looked like a monster. "Who am I?" I wondered. It seemed I had lost myself years ago. With this unpleasant feeling, I put the spoon in the sink.

I tried to understand Martin, tried to understand why he had become so furious this morning. I made an effort to see him as a separate being. Our relationship had welded us together in a most uncomfortable way. I could hardly imagine him having had an existence of his own before we met.

I stopped scrubbing the frying pan and let it slide into the dishpan. I stared into the gray water, and suddenly remembered a camping trip where Martin had given me warmth and affection. I saw him standing in a clearing all by himself, sunshine around him. But immediately my bitter feelings rushed against the image and washed it away.

I tried again. This time I saw Martin's father; his stern features, his mouth with his strong healthy teeth. Suddenly the old man's upper jaw grew into a long flat snout edged with teeth, and he turned into a swordfish that was charging and snapping at his son. As the image disappeared, it flared through my mind: Martin must be so bruised! But my own hurt was too painful to have much concern for his.

At this moment the door opened. We both started. Usually, before someone came in, you could hear the clatter of their skis being taken off and their stomping on the porch to get rid of the snow.

A young fellow was standing in the doorway. The cold air was rushing in and I thought, "Is he ever going to close that door?" Finally, he did, stepped in the dining room and walked awkwardly to a table and sat down. He was eighteen at the most , blond hair sprouting on his chin. He ordered a coke in a brisk voice. When I brought it to him, I asked if he cared for some hot soup. "No, no soup," he said. The way he refused shocked me. It was not so much the rudeness, but the distress in his voice. "What is wrong with this kid?" I wondered.

The telephone rang. Martin got up and answered. This surprised me because usually, even when he was standing close by, I had to get it, no matter what I was doing. This small act of his told me that he was ready to make peace. I heard Martin saying, "You can't expect me to remember all the guests we had today...just my wife and me...no, they all left except one who came in just now..."

I heard a noise and turned around. Never in my life have I seen someone move so swiftly: the young fellow practically flew through the room, yanked the receiver from Martin, put it on the hook; and in the next moment, both were on the floor; Martin bumping his head on the counter when he fell. The kid was on top, holding Martin down.

For a long moment I could neither think nor act. Then something became clear: I was not afraid! Right in front of me was violence—not the vague threat of it that had hung over me so long. And now suddenly, when it had become real, I felt the opposite of fear: a feeling of excitement, of exhilaration began filling me.

I looked for a weapon. I wanted my frying pan, but I could not see it. I had forgotten that it was soaking in the sink. I went to the stove and got a good round log. I can't remember if I was undecided for a second whose side I was going to take; I don't think I was. I went up to the wrestling and panting men, aimed and knocked the stranger over the head, once, twice. Not too hard, but hard enough to make him all limp for a moment, long enough for Martin to get out from under and on top of him, and for me to run to the workshop and come back with a piece of rope. Together we bound his hands behind his back. I could see how upset and angry Martin was, because he pulled the rope much too tight.

I asked, "Was this a cop you talked to?" Martin nodded, still out of breath. I called the police back.

The road was barely passable, but two policemen arrived shortly. They handcuffed the lad, and I was glad to see the tight rope coming off his wrists. He handled the interrogation well, just answering some basic questions, keeping silent about everything else.

When they were ready to leave, I opened the door for them. It was snowing hard and already a thin new layer was covering everything. The policemen looked worried.

"It won't be easy to stay on the track."

"I know the road well, every bit of it," Martin said, "I'll go down with you and drive. I don't mind staying in the village overnight." The two men looked relieved.

After they left, I went outdoors too, to watch the snow falling. As far as the porch light reached, I saw the flakes twirl down, thousands and thousands. I opened my palms where they settled gently, and I watched them melt away. They fell on my forehead and nose and caressed my cheeks. They landed on my lips and I licked them away and tasted them.

Back in the house I heard the flames crackling, the fire was going good. I felt alive, like a person again. It was wonderful. But something still needed to be done.

I took Martin's coffee cup from the shelf. I held it in my hands for a moment. It was a ceramic cup with a white and gray glaze. I said quietly, "It is not you Martin, but it is your behavior that I cannot stand." I took a deep breath and threw the cup against the stove. There was a dry, low sound, then two deeper ones when it bounced to the floor tiles, and a high ring at the end. Like shots I thought. Then silence again. The cup had broken into two parts. I picked them up and fitted them together. Nothing was missing. I went to the garbage and dropped the pieces in.

The next morning, as soon as the ski-lift had resumed its humming and clicking, Martin returned. From then on our relationship improved a little. But it was still hard for me to live with him. We had supported each other's weakness for too long—I, his oppressive behavior, he, my unassertiveness—and when spring came, we separated.

The young fellow was set free; they could not prove he had committed the crime he was accused of. I have forgotten what it was. Sometimes I wonder what happened to him.

Other men came into my life and left again. I didn't know what I wanted. It was not marriage.

The day arrived when it became clear to me that I needed more space and different experiences than what I could find in my home country. I had to break away from my present life, say goodbye to family, friends, workplace and country.

I dragged an overseas trunk down from the attic in my parents' house. My grandfather had used it when he sailed to the United States as a young man a hundred years before me. His trunk was still good and useful but I knew I would experience another America than the one he described in his diary. What was awaiting me there? I was sure it would be something good.

Things didn't move as fast as I wanted. "You'll have to wait for at least two years before we can give you the visa," they told me at the American Embassy. I decided to make a detour and go to South America first.

My first night on the freighter I was standing on the deck. The moon was shining and threw a silver band across the sea. Boldly the ship moved ahead. I bent over the railing and gazed into the black water. It foamed and flowed backwards. The big, cold "No" of the moon frightened me. Down below, the sea suggested gently to give myself up. To others on the boat I may have looked free and strong but I was not. I fled into my cabin. Gradually I got used to the life on board and the slow, long journey became exciting and wonderful.

We landed at a few places and I marveled at this new world I was entering. Finally we reached Peru, my destination, and I settled in the capital.

I liked Lima and felt accepted by the big city as by a friend. I especially loved her evenings: an orange glow settles on the houses, the woodwork, the faces of the people streaming through the narrow main street. They stand at the corners, sit on the balconies, sleep in the squares. They are all transfigured by the evening light. The humid, mellow air is full of longing. Crowds of people pass La Merced. Swift fingers mark the sign of the cross on forehead and chest. There is a blissful smile on the rococo façade of the church. It soothes the sorrows and sufferings of the passers-by. It warms my heart, too.

I felt almost at home in Peru. I found work, found friends, I saw magnificent scenery and received glimpses of a baffling pre-history. But I was lonely even though I fell in love easily and often, and then one day, seriously. Just then I received my visa for the United States. I decided to depart and travel by land. I said goodbye and left the country. I felt like crying.

The Thief

THE TRAIN WAS PUSHING ITS WAY through the jungle, dragging clouds of black smoke behind it. It had been unbearably hot all day long. Everyone was exhausted. They stirred only to wave a newspaper or a hat in front of their faces.

The slow ride on the train was interrupted by another stop. Except for a few huts there was nothing to see. Suddenly two men appeared from the forest. One of them with a machete in his hand was running after a youth who, wild with fear, rushed toward the train. He jumped into our car, yelling for help, screaming, "He is going to kill me!"

At this, the drowsy silence breaks into pieces. Everyone jumps to their feet. There are shrieks, there is turmoil. Some men block the door to keep the one with the knife from entering. The lad is on his knees, he is wringing his hands, he is sobbing, quivering, begging just for a ride to the next station to save his life. He implores all the saints. The conductor comes in, tells him to get off the train as his adversary has promised not to harm him and, addressing the passengers, states "He is a thief, he has stolen money." The lad is led off the train. The ride goes on. The passengers drop back into their seats. Soon conversation ceases.

At last the sun disappeared. Dark, sad, with heavy outlines the trees stood before the glowing sky. The world was filled with moisture like tears. Creation was still going on, like a stirring in the sleep, an attempt to awaken. I glanced at the passengers. All those faces were new and unknown to me. I felt I had already been living for a long, long time and was going to outlive them all. Was I a thief stealing from them, years of experiences, stealing material wealth? I didn't understand my feelings, and didn't want to think about them.

After three months of traveling I reached the United States border and saw the Star Spangled banner fluttering. I felt some of the awesome power behind that flag. Would they let me cross? A couple of hours later I sighed with relief. They had let me in. Hurray!

I found perfect roads, fast buses, efficiency all over. I got off in San Francisco. The city was cold, the people unsmiling. I didn't like it. I'll stay here a year or two then move on to Japan or return to Europe, I thought.

But there was a vitality around me that grabbed me. The freeways with their generously curved on and off ramps became for me the symbol of a free flowing, aggressive life. I was encouraged to follow it. I could develop anything I had inside me. I could see no barriers. Finally here was the space I had craved without clearly understanding it. Slowly I began unwrapping myself from my cocoon and becoming more accepting of myself and of others.

Someday I knew I wanted to do the most creative act I was capable of: giving birth, and raising a child. "I can get married later," it occurred to me. At the international student house of the university there was always a crowd of intelligent, handsome people going in and out. Suddenly in my thirties men became attracted to me. There must be times in our lives when we feel completely safe, can let go of our controls and be open to what the universe wants to give us. Totally miraculous things may then happen. I felt that was the case when my children came to be.

Shadows and fears tend to come back into our lives. Family life was not easy for me. But children will grow up anyhow. Mine were born into a culture that was valid for them but foreign to me. This country became theirs and they were shaped by its qualities and its failures.

The Press Release

THERE WERE THREE SCHOOL AGE GIRLS in the room, and their mother. The oldest girl was sitting at the table, papers and books spread over it. She said, "You know what's worst is going to school on cold rainy days." She spoke softly in a slightly depressed tone. "Actually the rain is not so bad, just the cold and gray."

On the other end of the room the second oldest was sitting curled up in the corner of the couch, holding a notebook on her knees. She called over to the oldest, "Julia, are you almost done with your report? Can I read it?"

"It's not *near* done," Julia answered.

"Can I read it after?"

"Yeah," Julia answered condescendingly.

"God, I wish I knew if Harriet Tubman..."

"Mom, Mom," the youngest interrupted in her full resonant voice. She was sitting on the couch, too, with a newspaper on her lap. "Listen to this, it is gross." The second one chimed in, talking quickly and nervously. "Mom read it already, I saw her reading it."

Mother, reading a magazine and not really listening, interfered, saying in a conciliatory tone, "Lisa, let Mary Lou read it to me if she wants to."

Without waiting a moment Mary Lou began, "Kelsey goes coolly to his death."

"You read it, Mom, I've seen you read it," Lisa screamed, her voice tense, barely hiding her anxiety.

Mary Lou went on undisturbed. "They dropped eggs? What, what cyanide eggs?" Lisa, realizing that she could not stop the reader, said sarcastically, "yeah, cyanic eggs. They pffff..."

Mary Lou, absorbed in the article, burst out, "Yuck, it says..."

Lisa stopped her for a second with "Cow."

Her sister began again slightly distracted, "It says...it says that...okay at 12:21 a.m. right? Ten minutes after the cyanide eggs were dropped into the acids..."

Julia's voice came from the other side of the room, "You know they have little cyanide birds..."

Mary Lou pulled herself together "'...causing deadly fumes...'"

Lisa added, "They go tweet, tweet."

"'To rise under the chair, metal chair. He was strapped onto...'"

Lisa tried once more to stop her sister. "I 'ready read it, Mary Lou." There was despair in her voice.

"...shoulders and okay, well, why did they do that?"

Lisa answered her, "Just so he wouldn't jump up and have a hangoutang."

Mary Lou slightly annoyed, "No, not that, I was wondering why they have those eggs, to make him conk out or what?"

Lisa soberly, "To kill him."

Mother, anxious to give an answer to her youngest, volunteered, "Maybe that's the way...instead of an electrical chair or a gas chamber?"

There was even more sarcasm in Lisa's voice when she saw her mother allied with the youngest. She said, "Yeah, they gassed him with eggs, ha."

Julia's voice became audible again, "With really rotten eggs."

Mary Lou went on, "Well, gawd, how gross, they even, they put it into detail, how he took several deep breaths," she hissed, "fff-fff."

Lisa again, yelling, "I read it, Mary Lou!"

Mother intervened weakly, "We don't have to hear that, Lisa."

"'After several minutes his body was motionless except for an occasional shudder.' You know why they put that because people always go," and here she changed her voice, deepened it and said dramatically, "Wow, this guy, dead, oh wow," and added, "That's gross."

Lisa asked, her voice suddenly gentle and soft, "Mary Lou, did you blow dry your hair?"

"Yeah, I dried it."

Julia called, "Mom, I need your help with my report."

"Okay, I'm coming."

Mary Lou, slightly disappointed that she was no longer the center, tried again hesitatingly, "Okay, let's see…"

But Lisa had had enough, "Shh, I cannot *work* with all you googoo heads talking."

"Mom, I *need* your help," Julia repeated.

How did it all happen so fast? My daughters finished school and left home. Those twenty years of raising children passed as though they were just one of the many episodes in my life, and seemingly a short one. I was alone again, had space, quiet and the chance to start all over with new experiences, new relationships. A long neglected "me" began to surface. Gradually I understood it was the part of me that wanted to write.

I love to take in the rich red-brown color of my tea. I inhale the aroma of those leaves that have absorbed the tropical sun for many months and now they are giving it forth, lavishly. When I exhale, the surface of the liquid trembles and the reflection of my face almost disappears in the little waves. From this angle my wrinkles and sagging muscles are exaggerated and give me a hint of how I'm going to look in ten years. I can study my face now without feeling pain because it doesn't come up to some kind of beauty standard. What a burden it was being young!

The first story I wrote after that long silence was about a friend who came into my life like a quiet visitor and ended up putting my whole being into disarray.

The Visitor

I WAS SITTING ON THE COUCH in my room watching the clock. Someone was supposed to come to see me that morning at eleven.

The objects in the room were hazy, having lost their substance. I had had an experience two days ago that threw me violently out of my routine. It ejected part of me out of my body, and left me suspended halfway into another reality.

I was waiting for Jean. One long hug she had given me had done it. I had never been in love with a woman, nor even thought about it, and now, when it had happened, the earth seemed to have stumbled in its course. There was only one safe place left to hold onto: Jean.

I wanted to recall her features; but, when I tried to see her face, the image of a huge cloud arose. I tried to visualize her person, and a giant winged creature appeared.

I had asked her to come to my house at eleven, but was this possible? And would she heal the pain I was in?

I had to collect my thoughts and concentrate on something. There was an Oriental rug on the floor. I tried to read its pattern and follow the repetition of its triangles, rhombi, and L-shapes. I didn't like the message it was giving me. It was saying, "What makes you think your feelings are so important and unique? You are but a tiny geometrical form in a big design; you have no voice in the scheme of the universe."

My eyes wandered off and stopped at an antique chair in the far corner. It had a balloon back and an upholstered seat. It once belonged to my grandmother. I wished my eyes could rest on modern furniture whose straight lines would lead me away, out of the window, away from this world. But those last century chairs with their rounded forms seemed to be so satisfied with their existence that their curved arms and legs would hug this planet forever.

When I was little, I would be sitting on—and sometimes under— a chair like this and it was fun to travel my fingertips along its grooves. I inspected the dust that had settled in the corners and hardened there. Sometimes I would close my eyes and glide my fingers along the chair's many grooves until I came to a stop. There was playfulness in this chair, but not enough, and it came to a stop so suddenly. I was disappointed. And I would ponder about the person who had made this chair and about grown-ups in general. My life then was full of stops and limits set up by adults. Had I finally left that narrowness behind me and stepped into a wider circle?

It was still not eleven. I got up from the couch. I felt I was not getting enough air. My body was hurting as though there were tight clamps all over my arms and around my organs inside. I knew I could only be rid of this pain if I could hang on close to Jean, bury my body inside hers.

I walked over to the rubber plant. It looked good, those half dozen leaves against the white background of the wall. The leaves were so simple and unstructured. I touched one of them and felt its cool smoothness. A memory stirred inside me, of not being quite awake, of sadness, of heavy tears. The jungle...

How long ago was it, when I decided to flee the restrictive environment where I grew up, and sail to South America? Then there I was. Inside all the richness, the abundance of water, amplitude of the sky, greenness without end. The white lancha is floating down the Ukayali river. Now refreshing rain draws across the river like a gray wall and makes the shores vanish. When the boat lands, the sailors jump into the shallow water, climb up the slope, dragging the rope behind them. Naked feet disappear in the wet sand. Feet run across the soft grass up the hill.

Now the boat stops where neither village nor houses can be seen. It is dark. Women step out of the bushes. They carry baskets and basins on their heads. They march across the narrow plank into the hold of the ship. The captain, lean and taciturn, is standing in their midst, bargaining for eggs and fruits. An electrical bulb gives some light. Though the figures fill the room, they leave it nearly empty. The expression of their faces is so vague that I'm afraid their consciousness might disperse any moment and merge into the big breathing of the jungle.

I had hoped to leave behind all the "no's" and "don'ts" which had restricted me at home. But they were inside me, and I had carried them along.

I remembered I felt lonely among those people, but lonely was just what I wanted to be. My eyes were wide open but my lips were closed tightly; I didn't want to reveal myself to anybody. I harbored a deep grudge against the adult world. I traveled on.

What happened that I had changed so much since then? I still could not believe the miracle that I had found a person—was it a person?—who was so vast, so deep, so understanding that I wanted to give myself up, share myself completely. I felt I was at the most crucial moment of my life. I wanted to touch her body, drink her body, drown myself in her body. But what if my feelings for her frightened her, what if she turned away from me? I could not bear the thought.

There was a knock at the door. In a second everything was back into focus. My fantasies had disappeared. I was not aware of my feelings. I walked to the door with the smile of a hostess. I opened it. Jean was outside; real and solid. She was several inches taller than I; long black hair, big intelligent eyes, a round face. She spoke; her voice caressed me. She entered. She was slightly disconcerted and did not hug me. She looked for a place to put her purse. Suddenly I hated her purse: this feminine article, this symbol of dependency and concern for details. A message flashed up: She is not free, she cannot love me! But I let it drift away from my mind.

Jean put her purse down and pulled me into a gentle hug. My body tensed up, I was not ready to let myself go. When we separated, she let her hand rest on my shoulder a moment longer. Her touch felt strong, just because it was so light and relaxed, allowing a hundred channels in her hand to open up, letting energy flow out. I felt the trickle in my shoulder. She was a healer and a leader and I needed her so much.

We sat down on the pillows on the floor. Silence. I knew I should talk, say what I wanted to say. I wished my throat didn't feel so tight, like it was being strangled. Then could I convey by means of words the feelings which overwhelmed me; could I translate them into this gray, limited, reality? I felt more and more depressed. How could I tell Jean that I loved her and that this body of mine wanted that body of hers?

Suddenly that special P.E. class came to mind, one that I had had to take as a teenager to strengthen my posture. I did not know why I was not holding myself straight. It was embarrassing to have to take that class.

The lights are on in the huge, unfriendly hall. I am cold and my hands are red and purple and I want to hide them. I know something is wrong with me.

And now this feeling about my body came back: I didn't have a solid body like everyone else! Jean did not seem to notice. Yet she had so much presence herself. What kind of support and nourishment did she get as a child that I did not? Surely she did not grow up in a vacuum like I did. There was no touching in my family, and all communication happened at a distance not closer than three feet. There was a danger zone around my parents. It was wider around my father than around my mother, and there seemed to be an invisible sign that read: "No trespassing."

I felt like saying to Jean, "I know my body is insignificant and almost non-existent, but still, it must be real." I exhaled, it came out like a sigh.

"You want to tell me something?" Jean said and took hold of both of my hands. I looked into her eyes. They seemed even bigger now; they were widening and their rims seemed to overflow, as though they wanted to reach me, to envelop and cradle me. And still I could not talk.

I let go of her hands. I could not accept this gesture of sympathy, of a rational friendship. Rather I wanted to pull her down inside my desperation, the uproar of my feelings. But suddenly I did talk. I could hear my voice coming out thin, fragile, hoarse, and, unable to carry my feelings into this world of air and three dimensions.

"I love you, Jean, I love you so much all of a sudden; I have not felt like this in half a lifetime."

Jean was looking attentively at me, "You mean sexually, too?"

I nodded, "Yes."

"Let's go over there to the couch and cuddle together." I followed her in a daze. We lay at each other's sides, our bodies hardly touching; our hands resting lightly on each other's shoulders. Gradually my body began to relax, to heal.

I felt I was surrounded by the ocean. It was a deep blue, brilliant and immense. A boat was rocking on the waves. It reminded me of a picture of Noah's ark. It was made of warm brown wood. Its sides bulged out beautifully, voluptuously. Sometimes it floated close by me, sometimes it was farther away, rocking in the sunshine.

"What are you thinking?" Jean asked.

"Thinking? I was half-dreaming."

"You said you have not had these feelings for a long time?"

"Yes, I haven't felt this kind of love since I was in my twenties. But some of it goes back further..the pain...it has something to do with my mother."

"Tell me about you, when you were a child, and about your mother."

"My mother was very strict with me, and she was hard to approach. I was so powerless..."

Now I'm small again. I'm standing in front of my toy chest, emptying all my belongings out and enjoying them.

I'm aware that there are other people in the house. And I'm aware that we live in two different realities. One is a solid and square world of the adults which is getting more important every day. Superimposed on this, there is another. It is a sphere, and we live inside of it. It has a shadowy, soft quality. In this sphere we are tied together with dark velvety bands. They connect all of us so that when one person moves, or rather when that person's mood shifts, it is transmitted to all of us immediately.

My parents don't have faces. My father moves through the sphere as a dark figure surrounded by a gentle, low-burning, blue light. My mother is all red and orange, violent flames burst from her frequently. When she holds me close, the burning around me is spectacular.

Inside the square world, my mother is usually friendly and holds back all strong emotions. But I'm never sure when the dam is going to break. I see her coming into the room now, with a tray of dishes to set the table. She notices that I have left my toys on the dinner table, or maybe that, inadvertently, I have spilled a little water on the waxed floor. Suddenly there is a sea of hostility. Her words pelt me and make me ache inside. I withdraw, heavy with guilt and shame.

I said aloud to Jean, "I hated her, I was afraid of her, but mostly, I felt an intense love for her." I felt Jean's hand gently stroking my shoulder.

I saw myself growing older. The sphere disappeared, and I did not see lights around people anymore. I forgot about it. There was now a cold, hard iron fence around my mother. She had locked me out, and I was angry. Even the thought of breaking through that gate was too terrifying to consider. I did not know that I was building an identical fence around myself, trying hard not to show my feelings to anyone any longer. Tucked away in my mind there was the recollection of a state of deep contentment with another human being. Dimly I recalled the touching of my mother's hands when I was very young. Her hands were small, but muscular, and well-proportioned. Long before I noticed their physical appearance, I experienced a blue light emanating from them. It was different from the one that surrounded my father. It was stronger denser, bluer. When she touched me, I was led back to an initial existence of bliss, to a time when there was no pain and no separateness.

And there was another gift she gave freely. Her hands were made to build and form. There was wisdom in them. Beautiful thoughts flew out of her hands. I could see them as forms that were white, bright, elegant, and they played around me like butterflies.

Suddenly I felt annoyed that my mother suppressed her talent, that she worked hard to be a housewife and mother in order to live up to society's expectations of her. It occurred to me that sometimes her sacrifice was too heavy to bear, and her pain turned into hostility against the ones around her.

I said to Jean, "If only my mother had developed her creative abilities, instead of keeping house!"

There was a smile on Jean's face, but soon it disappeared and turned into a sigh, "If only it were so easy..."

I became aware of something, and it seemed like a miracle that this person at my side, whom I loved so much, had gone through the same experiences as I, tried the same almost impossible task of raising children in the isolation of a suburban house and nuclear family. She had struggled and suffered like I had! I threw my arms around her neck and kissed her forehead and her cheeks again and again.

"It's not easy, I know..." I lay down.

Old memories came up again. I see my children. They are babies and we all live in a white wooden house. I'm standing in the kitchen trying to attend to some housework. The children are crying and want my attention. One is clinging to my clothes, the other has draped herself around my leg. And there is a third one somewhere. They are hanging to me so tight that I cannot move...

For a time I had enjoyed having and raising children. But gradually what had been a pleasure—taking care of them— had become a duty, and I felt I was chained to the house. My work had become an unpleasant routine, and, when I entered the supermarket, I felt nauseated. My husband had turned into a person who meant only more demands, more attention giving, and I dreaded his return in the evening. All week I would look forward to the one afternoon when I could take off by myself. My husband's face hardly concealed his unwillingness to take care of the children on his free day. They wailed when I left because they had become so dependent on me.

Finally, I closed the door behind me. I could not hear the children crying anymore. All the pressure was gone and I almost broke into tears. I walked down the streets. I saw all the people going by so purposefully. A world existed outside of my house, but I did not belong to it. I had no place to go, no business to attend to. I felt I was excluded from the real world forever.

Of course there were friends I could have gone to. Friends with husbands and children, friends living in their little houses like I did. But either they pretended everything was all right with their lives, or they really believed it. I could not share my despair with them. What I needed were people who hugged me, not because I was a wife or a lover or a mother, but because I was a human being with needs of my own.

Sometimes I would get up when it was still dark outside, take the dog and go to the beach. I could smell the ocean and hear the waves before I could see them. Down on the sand I took off the dog's leash, and immediately he flew away like an arrow and disappeared in the dark. Then he came back still racing, and he seemed so happy that finally he was free and could let go of his pent-up energy. And he would bark at the waves or sniff and dig in the piles of seaweed that were lying around.

I watched the morning come with all its lovely pastel colors in the sky and on the water. The scenery was like a display in a store window; it was beautiful, but it was not for me. I could hear the pounding of the waves but my heartbeat had nothing to do with it. It was not an echo. The breeze went around me, but it did not touch me. I only knew that I had a body because it shivered, shivered.

Reluctantly I put the dog on his leash. He was a strong animal and hard to control. I returned to my house, to that sad place, but it was home.

I was standing in the kitchen with the children crying and clinging to me, and on the stove the soup was boiling and had to be stirred. All that the children needed was a hug and a moment of my attention. But it seemed there was nothing left I could give them. And, besides, the soup had to be taken care of. For some reason this was important. The things in the house had to be orderly and under control. I saw the predicament of my children, but I could not let my feelings come to the surface. It was too dangerous to give the love they needed because, if I gave in, a surge of other feelings would rise. I would burst. I would shatter this existence. I would run through the streets and yell, "I cannot live this way anymore! Help! I can't bear being locked up inside that house any longer!" Or I would get in the car, drive away with a roaring engine and never come back again. I was not ready yet.

I took one step forward. One child let go, sobbing. I took another step forward. The other child, who was hugging my leg, fell backwards, bumped her head on the floor and screamed in frustration. Quietly, as though nothing had happened, I stirred the soup, lowered the heat. Then I turned to the children, picked them up mechanically, chided them for being so impatient and seated them at the table.

I opened my eyes. My daydreams made me feel sad, and old feelings of guilt emerged.

I said to Jean, "How many times was I mean to my children and played the role of the fairy tale stepmother? It is true that I was isolated from other women, cut off from the rest of society, felt useless and depressed half of the time, but still..."

"Remember," Jean said softly, "you did the best you could. We women have to work together for change and create a world where people are free to be themselves and free to love." She talked to me a long time. The sound of her voice was miraculous to me. It reminded me of earthen bowls holding water. They clinked together and rang with a muted joyfulness.

I said to her, "Sometimes now I feel I'm beginning a new phase, I suddenly have a vision of a more encompassing circle. It was so different yesterday, when I walked through town. Suddenly I saw the women! Before, I was mostly aware of the men; the women were less meaningful, less visible. But overnight they have emerged, alive, powerful and turned into future friends, allies, lovers. The potential for love has doubled. I still can't get over it, it's so wonderful—and it's all because of you!"

"You are special to me, too," she whispered and drew me closer. She left her hand firmly on my shoulder, and I felt this was all the closeness she wanted.

It was strange to be so near an unfamiliar body. I had to learn so much. It was like a message that reached me by way of subtle vibrations, colors, smells. Lying there quietly, I learned and learned.

"I lived in South America before I came here," I said. "I spent some time in the jungle, traveled on the rivers. I'll never forget that time. You must know that I grew up amongst trembling birch trees, rocks, pale sunsets; but there—I can't describe it—the abundance; the richness; the colors," and I added softly, "You, too, there is something about you: your body, your hair. It's soft, moist, alive...the jungle," and my hand went to rest under her thick black hair.

We stayed like this until Jean gave a restless stir, and I knew she wanted to get up.

"It feels so good to be with you," I said and I bent over her face.

She pulled my head down and our lips touched. I had to move back; I didn't want the longing of my body to come to the surface.

"I love you, Jean."

"I love you, too." Her reply was so immediate it almost hurt.

She used the same words, but what she meant was different. We separated and got up. I wondered about her words. There was caring in her words, but no desire. What would our relationship be? Would it last?

A last short hug "I'll be seeing you," and the door closed behind her.

I was alone in the familiar room, standing on the Oriental rug, seeing my grandmother's chair, the potted plants. Everything in the room was trying to give me its message—but I did not listen. Somebody seemed to be standing at my side, taller than me, stronger. Was it the memory of Jean's presence, or was it a new form of myself?

Women friends: they carried me gently in their arms from one stage of my life to the next.

I remember Hannah, my oldest friend. She came to my house for the first time when we were seven years old. I asked her politely if she wanted to play with the dolls because I knew lots of girls liked that. She declined equally politely. I was glad. From then on we just talked and left the toys alone.

How much poorer my life would be without Elvira. When I go to her home, I always settle in her huge arm chair. I forget if she got it from the Salvation Army or if she picked it up at the roadside, then covered it with a handmade throw. She says to me simply and unhurriedly, "Erika, and how are you?" Her words make me relax at once. I feel I have the permission to be myself and her caring envelops me in layers of soft blankets.

Selma has a delicious body. It's strong like a tree trunk but padded so nicely and covered with a warm, brown skin. A couple of times we curled up together and made love. I wonder if she still thinks of me.

Some of my friends moved away, others moved out of this world. Like June. She made delicious parsley soups while fighting cancer. One day she called up to say good-bye in her usual cheerful voice. "I would like to come back for awhile as a dolphin and frolic around the water. If you see any playing in the waves, think of me."

Lydia's green eyes pulled me into her mysterious world. Baskets full of warm colored yarns stood in her living room. She created intricate objects that matched the complexity of her thoughts. She went on a long trip by car and never returned.

There was another one I lost who did not die nor did she move far away.

The Vigil

WE WERE ALL SITTING in Bridget's living room, waiting. Ann was crocheting, holding a heap of colored yarns on her lap. Bridget and Susie were talking, or rather it was Susie who talked while Bridget sat silently, almost rigidly, in a straight-backed chair. Susie's teenage son was sprawled on the couch, his feet propped up on his sleeping bag. I had a book in my lap, not because I felt like reading but because I did not feel like talking to anyone, least of all to Bridget. I did not want to be where I was.

When I look back to that scene, it seems that the living room was huge and empty when in fact I know that the upholstered furniture was so close together that Jacob, when he walked by later in the night, kicked those teenage legs as if by mistake before Larry could pull them back. The walls were not bare at all but lined with shelves that were packed with records and books.

It all began in the afternoon of that same day. I was sewing on the porch and Susie, a neighbor, was keeping me company. Suddenly Bridget walked up to us, her two little daughters behind her. I was so surprised to see her here that at first I did not notice how upset she was. She never visited me nor did she call. For a moment I was delighted that finally she had come to see me.

"I'm awfully sorry to disturb you," she said, "but I have to talk to you for a moment."

Bridget's daughters spotted our swing and headed for it immediately.

I introduced the two women to each other and I finally realized how distraught Bridget was, too nervous to settle in a chair.

"Jacob is getting worse. We had a terrible fight earlier today. He became physical for the first time. He is threatening me. He is out now, but he'll return tonight. I'm scared to be alone with him at night. Could you come and stay with me?"

I realized at once that this was serious. Bridget never asked for help nor did she talk much about her marriage. I did not like to be pulled into a conflict with her husband and I was also afraid. But because she was a friend of mine and was in distress, I said, "Sure, I'll stay with you, if that's what you want. But why don't you stay here with your children instead. We have enough space and it's safer."

Bridget gave me some reasons why she wanted to go home, like being afraid he would lock her out for good, or not wanting to be a run-away wife. None of these reasons seemed compelling but it wasn't the moment to argue. She agreed, however, to leave her daughters with my mother and with my own children.

Susie asked if it would be helpful for her to come too, and be another support person tonight.

"Sure," Bridget agreed, "That's awfully nice of you."

"Ah, goody," Susie said with a beaming face.

Though I was glad to have another person with me, I also disliked Susie's enthusiasm. She seemed to look forward to the night as if it were to be an exciting adventure and she seemed to carry a banner, "We women have to stand up for each other!"

We agreed to be at Bridget's house at eight, half an hour before Jacob was expected to be home.

I began thinking about the time when I heard him singing in the church—a lone figure by the altar, his voice, mellow and vulnerable, traveling effortlessly through the room. He sang Dvorak's Biblical Songs.

> "Lord, hear my fervent pleading...
> Full of fear my heart is beating,

> Cold shudders of death seize me,
> Dread befalls me..."

I had been moved, and I admired him for being able to create so much beauty and stir everyone's emotions. Later I met him at Bridget's house. Even close up he was handsome with his black hair, pale skin, a little overweight. He seemed older than her and there was something fatherly about him, something dependable. He was polite but unwilling to engage in a conversation. He was leaning against a pole, one foot braced against it, gazing over the lake. They were fortunate, I thought, a comfortable house right at the lake. What else could one want?

If I thought they had no worries, I was mistaken. Bridget explained to me some time ago, "Jacob torments himself because of his voice. There is a strange hoarseness that sometimes suddenly appears before a concert. The sound won't come out, it is like a stutter." She continued, "He had to cancel a couple of concerts at the last minute. He is afraid for his career."

"Does he do anything about it?"

"Of course. He is seeing some of the best specialists in the country. They can't find anything wrong with his throat. He is convinced that he needs surgery, but they advise him to see a psychiatrist."

"Does he go to one now?"

"Him? Jacob? Never."

He must be under so much stress, I thought, and afraid of losing his voice altogether. Bridget said no more.

I decided not to change clothes. I expected to have to sleep on a couch or on the floor. I still remember I was wearing beige pants and a gray-blue shirt. The next morning when I came home, the first thing I did, was to stick my clothes in the washing machine. But even after they came out of the dryer they still seemed to radiate all the evil and ugliness of that night and I never wore them again.

When I arrived at Bridget's house, Susie was already there and just in case we needed some more protection, she had brought along her son Larry, and Ann, a friend of hers whom I knew also. This was disturbing and not what I had expected. I thought about leaving but I didn't.

Finally we heard a car, then the garage door. Jacob stepped in. For a moment he looked baffled and said, "Is this a kind of a party?" Then he addressed Bridget, "Tell your guests to go home." He went into the kitchen.

Nobody moved or said anything. After a couple of minutes he came back out, "I don't want any bums in my house." He picked up someone's purse and coat, opened the front door and flung the objects out on the lawn. No response.

He climbed the carpeted stairs that led to the split level and to his bedroom. Ann put her yarns on the floor, got up and retrieved her coat and purse. Susie engaged her in conversation. Larry pulled a well fingered book out of his backpack and started to read.

Bridget was sitting there quietly. I looked at her, at her thin boned frame, her big eyes. I realized whenever I hugged her, I always did it gently as though I were holding a delicate bird. She was depressed often and I felt like protecting and guarding her. I wanted to be close to her, but she never opened up, and the poetry she wrote, she never shared.

I kept on trying. She liked me to come and visit her, I knew this for sure. But I felt she did not see me as I really was. She idealized me, pretended that I could do no harm. Did she feel so badly about herself that she needed to make a kind of do-gooder out of me?

I liked her radical ideas, especially about feminism. She was well read and articulate. But I missed a real dialogue, a give- and-take. When I asked her a personal question, there was this silence around her. She did not reply for a few seconds and when she finally did, her first words blurted out too loudly and too abruptly as though it were difficult to get in touch with herself. Inside of her there seemed to be an empty space around the core of her personality while from the outside, depression squeezed her like a giant fist. I wanted that bare space, that part of her which she did not acknowledge, to become alive and burst open like a meadow in spring. I thought about all this until Jacob came down again.

"It smells here," he said, walking between us and kicking Larry's legs. He pulled the window wide open. The cold air from the lake streamed in.

"Why don't you go home now. Are you all on public assistance and don't have to work tomorrow morning?" He glowered at Susie, then Ann. "You there, you look like a streetwalker. Taking a night off, eh? And you, are you knitting an altar piece for the synagogue?"

It hadn't taken him long to discover that Ann was Jewish.

"Her over there," pointing to me. "She is the only one here who finished high school. You stupid drop-outs!"

He went upstairs again. We closed the window.

I thought then how could Bridget have lived with such a man for eight years? I remembered that she had confided in me that in case of a divorce she would lose her home and that she could not live without it. It was strange and annoying to me to see her trapped and so passive in life, when on the other hand her mind was sharp enough to cut through any problem that could be solved intellectually.

And there was this other riddle about Bridget I couldn't solve. We were once in a restaurant lingering over a meal. She was stirring some ice cubes with her fingers in the glass. The lemon slice rocked like a boat on the whiskey. We talked about African sculpture and I made some kind of generalization. After all, we were having a pleasant chat and not a scientific discussion. But all of a sudden she lashed out at me with hard words, accusing me of racism and who knows what else. It was clear that she wanted to hurt me and would have picked up any remark I had made or not made. Why had she hurt me on purpose? Why did she do that? I cried on the way home and did not call her for a long time. When I finally did, she apologized and blamed her drinking for her abusive behavior.

That silence around her, that gap in our conversations, I saw it differently now, sitting in her house. I sensed that space filling up slowly with a black ominous fluid which Bridget materialized and drew out with the power of her thoughts. From this point on I would tread very carefully in her presence.

After a while Jacob came down again dressed in elegantly striped pajamas. He strode through our midst pulling the window open furiously. His insults became sexual. He accused us of being lesbians and from the way he said it this was the depth of disgrace. He proceeded to discuss every part of our bodies, trying to vilify them and fantasizing what we were doing to each other and to his wife. Larry, too, was not spared. Jacob departed upstairs again and soon we heard him snoring. The others talked with animation to each other but I did not listen.

I was remembering that Bridget had hinted at sexual aberrations of Jacob's, that he felt very guilty and was scared to death that it might come out some day. I thought, no wonder his voice gets stuck in his throat sometimes.

The night dragged on. What were we doing here in this living room? Of course we wanted to protect Bridget and were still doing this or pretending to. But the situation had become askew in some way. I tried to figure it out but I could not think clearly. I was too upset by the situation and the verbal abuse I had endured.

Soon Bridget had fallen into her silence again. Her quietness was more than the absence of words. What was it? Words inside a negative space? Energy swelling inside a black hole? For the first time I admitted to myself that I was afraid of her.

Jacob appeared three more times. Each time he was refreshed and pelted his insults out more vigorously and more viciously. When he came out of his bedroom the third time and stood at the top of the stairs, everyone froze.

"He has a gun!" someone shouted. We jumped up.

"Just wait! I'll get you all!" he said threateningly.

I had known the gun was in the house. Bridget was afraid of burglars and at night she kept it loaded near her bedside. The gun didn't scare me too much. Jacob could not possibly shoot. He was angry but not desperate. His weapon was just another proof of his weakness, another way to intimidate us and make us leave.

A gun has a power of its own. It makes some hands tremble which are holding it, others it infuses them with the power they have been longing for. What would it do in Jacob's hands? Was I too naive in assuming he would not shoot?

It was months later at the trial when the subject of the gun was brought up again. Suddenly the judge who was obviously bored and had been scratching his ear with a pencil, stopped and became alert. He asked many questions, how many shots were fired, how far away and so forth. The eyes of the jurors, too, became alive and focused at once.

That night no shots were fired. I was glad when Susie left to call the police from a neighbor's house. The two policemen were young and felt visibly awkward in a situation they did not understand. Here we were, a motley group of women and a rumpled teenager, while Jacob—dressed in a fine silk robe—greeted them in the manner of a perfect gentleman. He handed over his gun. It was close to daybreak then.

Early in the morning Jacob came down and left without a word. We dispersed, too, though not without trying to persuade Bridget to move out and stay with one of us, but in vain. However, she was finally ready for a divorce and we found her a lawyer that same day.

During the following weeks I was out of town and was not in touch with Bridget. I knew the other women were there to help if needed. One day, while I was away, I received a long distance call from a friend. He said, "Do you know that Bridget shot Jacob?"

I stammered, "Is he dead?"

"Yes."

My first feeling was relief. Jacob's tortured soul is free. In my mind I saw him again in the church singing, "Save me, Lord, save me, Lord." It dawned on me that he perhaps wanted to die. Only a second later did I think about Bridget. A mass of thoughts rushed through my mind. "She has killed another human being—it's so dreadful I can't think about it—a hideous deed! She did it because she felt cornered, trapped with no way out. She will be treated as a criminal. What about her children?"

"He went after her with a crow bar," the voice on the phone said. "He came upstairs. She told him to stop or else she would shoot. He walked right on... The children are with Bridget's mother. I'll put you in touch with the lawyer," my friend added and hung up.

I saw Bridget again in the hall of the courthouse. She was pale and very thin but wore a cheerfully flowered skirt. She gave me a hug and thanked me profusely for coming. It felt as though I had come to her garden party and she was thanking me for helping serve the punch. But I understood that she was trying so hard to keep her real emotions down that she seemed insincere.

Susie was the first to testify. Before she entered the courtroom, she said to me, "She will be acquitted. After all, Bridget only acted in self-defense. The worst that could happen would be a conviction of involuntary manslaughter."

The hall where I was waiting was huge and empty. What if I said something wrong, something damaging to her? My hands were sweaty and I forgot to breathe. Finally I was called in.

Everything in the courtroom was hazy at first but I heard the lawyer asking me questions. While I answered, talking about my friendship with Bridget, I was feeling uneasy and remembering once when I was in a restaurant with her. She moved the ice cubes around in her glass then she stabbed me with her words. The lawyer was some distance in front of me. At my right side and out of the corner of my eye I could see the jurors and I sensed the mood that was coming from them. I felt non-acceptance, suspicion. I turned my head. I saw many tight-lipped, blank faces. They seemed to say, "You are whitewashing her, you cannot sway us, she is a criminal."

I said aloud, "Jacob made Bridget accountable for every penny she spent. Every night she had to submit her check book to him."

Did the jurors shrug their shoulders? Didn't they realize that this alone was hell?

"One day I babysat their daughters for a couple of hours," I went on, "When he came home and found out, he screamed at her and called her an irresponsible mother, leaving her children with a stranger."

Did the jurors nod their heads? Inside me I yelled, "Can't you understand that a mother cannot spend every second with her children? You fools, Bridget only shot her husband in self-defense. She had the same values as you. She believes in marriage and motherhood and status and the inability of women to make it alone in the world; that's why she did not get out of this marriage in time. On your terms she was perfect!"

"One last question," the prosecutor said, "Do you feel that Bridget ever loved her husband?"

Why did he ask this question? I wondered anxiously. All my arguments in favor of the defense crumbled. I did not know what to say. All I saw with my inner eyes was an airplane bursting into flames and falling. I knew it was because each time Jacob left for a trip Bridget hoped his plane would crash and he would never return. Had we both laughed when she told me?

"I cannot answer this question," I said.

Susie and Ann had gathered on my porch waiting for the jury's verdict.

"I don't think they will come to a conclusion today, I better go home," Susie said, but did not move from her chair.

"The judge, the prosecutor and the jury, all of them have those old fashioned ideas about marriage." Ann went on, "They think if both partners play their roles it works. If it doesn't, those men either have to get rid of their stale concepts or get rid of the defendant. They may choose the latter."

"If we all believe firmly that she will be acquitted then it will happen and we can have a party tonight," Susie said trying to inspire us.

The phone rang. We knew it was the lawyer. Both women followed me into the living room. When I picked up the receiver, I caught only three words clearly: second degree murder. I repeated them, "Second degree murder."

Susie fell into a chair and began to sob. Ann said over and over, "Those pigs, I didn't trust them."

I felt Bridget's life ended at that moment. She had years in jail ahead of her, one long drawn out death. I had not been able to protect her, protect her from herself. I put down the receiver.

I'm not turning on the light in the room. I want to watch the glow on the horizon and the darkness crawling out of the bushes and trees, and the slow numbing of meadows and hills.

The newspaper on the table is catching the last bit of light. The reports of crimes, injustices, looming wars are silenced now. This wonderful dusk is the only thing that is true for me at this moment.

I don't know when it happened. Months or years ago the world moved a little away from me and I became somewhat detached. I began to relax. With a sigh of relief I realized that I was not responsible for creating a perfect society in my life time. I came to believe that this world was just a short interlude, a place to practice and learn a few things.

So when I joined a demonstration against the production of nuclear weapons, I knew the real issue was not fighting the Bomb, but creating peace. By holding hands and moving and singing in unison we were helping each other to feel closer and diminish a little the separation between people. I believed that this separation was causing the shadows in this world.

The Blockade

WHEN I WOKE UP, my legs were numb with cold and I felt an unfamiliar surface under me. I opened my eyes. Lights were glaring on the wall below a row of windows. The sky was black. I closed my eyes again. The blockade, I'm in jail. I became aware of the hundreds of women sleeping around me. Their breathing was like a carpet of furry moss. Sleep is such a strange country, I thought.

I checked the blankets. Both were still over me and Michelle. We had pushed our cots close together so that we could share the covers. Her back was turned toward me, only a bushel of hair was sticking out from under the blanket. She could have been my daughter, age-wise, but I felt that she was more a mother to me with the acceptance and openness that radiated from her.

The events of the blockade two days ago reeled through my mind like a movie I had not turned on deliberately. I am in it again, my body shivering with cold and fear in the pre-dawn. A confusion of people, cars, policemen. Black clouds delaying the sunrise. "No Nukes" buttons, "Arms Are for Embracing," "Peace Is Possible." Black patrol cars rolling by slowly and menacingly. Policemen in riot gear, policemen on motorcycles. A sputtering helicopter above. Then suddenly the singing begins, like shiny glitter tossed into the air to transform the grim scene into joy and love.

Michelle grabs my left hand.

"Let's go!" She does not walk, she dances into the street, pulling me behind her. A sweaty hand takes my right. If we sing we won't get crushed. A blocked car with an uneasy driver inside; a woman trying to talk to him, asking him to turn around. My arms are being pulled back. Handcuffs feel tight. The sight of bound demonstrators makes my heart ache. A flock of chickens, ready for sale. I'm one of them. When the singing stops for a moment, feelings of fear and isolation invade me, but not for long. The singing resumes; it goes on forever. "The earth is our mother, we must take care of her..."

Someone close to me stirred and got up. Should I go to the bathroom now, before the lines form? I debated. On my way back I have to remember to turn right at the letter K on the "No Smoking" sign on the wall and then walk into the olive green ocean of cots and blankets, counting six rows. No, I won't get up yet.

The sky was illuminated by a faint gray. I felt the taut stretch of the canvas under my shoulder blades, under my buttocks; my arms were stretched out on my thighs to keep me warm.

Why am I here, why did I demonstrate? Is there a more subtle reason beyond the obvious one? I wondered.

Suddenly the lamps on the ceiling were turned on, and the light crashed down on us like a brutal truth. Moaning. A female voice through a bullhorn announced, "Good morning, ladies. It's time to get up. Breakfast will be ready in 45 minutes."

Bodies stirring; voices. Michelle turned around, stretched and sat up.

"Why are you here, Michelle, why did you let yourself get arrested?" I asked.

"Oh, me? Well, maybe to appreciate my own bed more," she said sleepily, "or maybe to be together with all these wonderful women here, the 'creme de la creme.'"

"Are both your parents French Canadian?" I asked.

"Yup. Why?"

"All that you need is a gilded frame around your head and you'd look like a portrait of some mistress at the court of

Louis XIV. But here, take my comb to look even more like that and before the other women ask for it. I feel like a capitalist here, not only owning a comb but also two pencil stubs and notepaper."

"I kind of believe in former lives, but then I see myself usually as a peasant digging the fields."

It's her eyes, I thought, her expressive gray eyes that seem to float freely in her face.

"You say that we in here are the cream of the cream," I continued, "but don't you think that there are many women here who protested for the sake of protesting no matter what the issue, and others who are here because they want to impress their boyfriends with their courage?"

"Maybe," she replied, "but that's all right. It's good for them; they will update their values. I know that there are millions outside who will join us when it's their turn. Now tell me, why are you here?"

"I'm trying to figure that one out. I didn't demonstrate during the Vietnam war," I said.

I remembered a classroom twenty years ago. A student mentions the march of the night before. A woman turns her head toward me, the teacher. She is pale, has dark hair. I like her. She wants an answer from me. "Why weren't you marching?" her eyes are questioning me. She does not know the pain I'm in, how it feels being locked up inside a capsule. I should have whispered in her ear, "Everywhere I go I feel like an outsider. I don't belong; that's why I cannot march with them."

My thoughts returned to Michelle and I said, "My upbringing made it hard for me to demonstrate when I was young. In the meantime I have dropped some of the shells that enclosed me. As to your question, 'Why am I here?' I'll tell you later."

"Look, the breakfast line is already longer than the bathroom line. We better go," she said.

"I can't get over it that they gave us a toothbrush and toothpaste," I said. "You don't even get that in a motel."

We walked along the cots and then along the side of the basketball court. Some women were doing yoga on its shiny wooden floor. We reached the end of the line.

A woman at my side said enthusiastically, "I enjoyed last night's ritual so much. It was almost worth going to jail just to be part of it."

Another one continued, "Wasn't it powerful when we screamed out our anger and fear? The dance at the end, too, was great."

"The food turns me off here," said a voice behind me, "when I see those giant pots, and the cooks filling their big ladles and slapping the food on your plate..."

A young woman I had never noticed before climbed on a table and announced, "There will be a general meeting at the center of the basketball court at 9 a.m. We'll have to decide in which order and under what conditions we want to be released."

She jumped down and disappeared into the crowd. I felt suddenly moved. All these leaders are popping up, I thought; then they vanish and others take over. It's wonderful.

I walked out of the gym, balancing my styrofoam and paper dishes, out into the sunshine, through low yellow grass, past groups of women who were eating, talking, resting. Ahead of me were the California hills, gently curved like sleeping animals, yellow now with dark tufts of oak trees clinging to them. Closer to me were decaying army barracks, barbed wire.

I placed my dishes carefully on the sand between the dry stubble. I sat down at the side of a gray-haired woman, attracted to her because she was one of my own generation.

She smiled at me, "No spills?"

"No," I replied, "I've mastered all the routines here already."

I looked into her gray eyes. What landscape is behind them? I wondered.

"What do you think," I asked. "Can we stop them?"

"Stop what? The nukes, you mean? It's a beginning. It takes time to change the consciousness of people."

The acid and astringent juice trickled down my throat.

"Somehow I feel that we are not doing enough," I said, "but I don't know what else we can do."

She nodded. "So far we have neglected to use most of our mental powers."

I looked at her, puzzled. She went on, "...realizing for instance that there are no enemies—disagreements, yes, but no enemies." Getting up, she added, "Also we have to visualize the kind of world we want to have in the future."

She spoke briskly as though she had a lot more to say. "I would like to talk more to you, but the meeting will start soon, and I want to sit in the middle of the circle to hear clearly what's going on."

I was disappointed when she left. I stirred my cereal and looked at its mountains and its valleys flooded with milk.

I envisioned the three politicians I disliked the most, sitting in front of me on a park bench. Then I imagined myself going and shaking hands with them, saying to each one of them, "Good morning. I just realized that you are a human being, too." Each time I stretched out my arm, I felt hatred, fear and disgust. The feelings were like bad creatures I had raised unknowingly, and they were now digging their claws into my stomach, snarling and not wanting to cooperate. It was strange. I was working for world peace but had forgotten to make peace inside myself.

When I had eaten, I got up and stuffed my paper plate and plastic ware into the already overflowing garbage can. I was drawn towards the tent where the showers were, as though I could wash off my unpleasant thoughts. Maybe I'll find Michelle there, I hoped.

The steam and the dim light made it hard to recognize anyone. Nude bodies were leisurely moving under the showers, letting themselves be caressed by the warm water that came gushing down in a luxurious spray. One woman was gently massaging another one who was lying on her stomach on a bench. Nearby, a young woman combed and untangled her friend's hair. This is like a vision of the future, I mused, a daily celebration of the body. I was tempted to skip the meeting, stay and abandon myself like the others, but I didn't.

A cluster of women had already formed on the basketball floor. I squeezed myself through until I found a small space to sit down. Low talking was going on. There was suspense like before a concert or a play. Who would be the actors, what kind of script? Would I be moved to participate? Someone far away waved. It was Michelle. I waved back.

Then suddenly, a woman raised her voice. "Who wants to be the facilitator?" Everyone became quiet at once. A hand rose. The meeting had begun.

I felt happy and comfortable inside this huge, dense clump of women. An unborn child must feel like this inside the womb of her mother, I thought, protected and cozy.

Could we come to a consensus to refuse to be set free unless the women and men who were jailed separately from us would be released at the same time? And how would we plead before the judge?

First the voices sounded calm and detached, but then, all of a sudden, ideas flashed from all over, and thoughts were thrown into the circle at a confusing speed. The proposals and agenda items accumulated like a heap of knotted strings, and the facilitator, with the help of some orderly and linear minds untangled them.

Moods swept the gathering. A feeling of power and exhilaration surged but then abated and turned into frustration and annoyance at each other. Accusations were heard, anger flared up and some voices sounded high and broken. The "vibes watcher" proposed that we break up into our affinity groups and deal with our feelings for a few minutes. The proposal was accepted.

I found Michelle and the other women who were from my town. The eight of us sat down cross-legged in a circle. Each one had a turn talking about her feelings. One of us screamed, "I'm so angry, so angry. There are still some sisters here who believe we can get anything by being nice and conciliatory. To hell with niceness." She pounded the floor with her fists. "Damn it, damn it, damn it."

Another woman spoke hesitatingly.

"I'm one of those who are for moderation in our demands. Perhaps you are right." She added softly, "It's just that I'm so much afraid of the men in power, of the whole system. Your energy gives me courage."

The one who, a moment before, had spoken angrily reached over and squeezed her hand. I looked at Michelle. A tear was flowing out of her eye. It lingered for a moment above her cheek, then ran quickly down her face. I felt a wave of love inside me.

Fifteen minutes later the seven hundred of us had gathered again, relaxed and calm. We had just started a new round of discussion when there was turmoil near the door. A woman rushed into the gym, heading toward us. Behind her, two armed guards followed. Everyone jumped up. I saw her squeezing into the middle of the gathering. Fear gripped me. I expected violence, hurts, punishment. At the shrill sound of a whistle, immediately more uniformed men came running in from the other side. Quickly women were holding hands, forming a circle around the fugitive, others encircled the guards.

"Sit down, sit down," the women shouted.

At once everyone was sitting. Somewhere "Om" was intoned and picked up by many voices. I saw a woman gently patting the back of a guard. He relaxed, let his arms sink. Now the gym was resonating with hundreds of voices, exhaling and chanting "Om, om, om." It seemed the vibrations created a shiny spiral around each body that circled rapidly, then rose. At each moment new spirals formed that circled, rose and played above our heads. We were creating a new structure around us, larger than the gym and not rigid, but undulating like the inside of a huge brilliant body.

The guards detached themselves. They walked out two by two, as though they needed each other. Two of them passed by me, their heads slightly bent as though their mother had chided them for wanting to use force.

The last "Om" came to a rest. We formed into a tight cluster again. We sorted out what had happened. Some women had stayed outdoors longer than most of us. Three of these were singled out by the guards as instigators, perhaps because they were more vocal and angrier than the rest. Suddenly two of them had been grabbed, cursed and led away while the third escaped and was now safe in our midst.

The meeting proceeded smoothly and finally consensus was achieved on all items.

I was sitting on my cot, Michelle at my side, drying her hair with a wet towel, radiating warmth from her moist body, warmth from her personality

And then the lawyers came in and announced that all our conditions for release were granted and that we would be brought before the judge and then set free in a matter of hours. There were cheers and an explosion of voices, motion, unrest.

Minutes later the two women who were led away earlier, entered the door and with them a few more who had been kept separate from us. More cheers and clapping and hugs.

I said to Michelle, "This morning you asked me why I came to jail. I think I know now."

She looked at me attentively, her eyes ready to receive my words and to absorb my mood and feelings.

"You remember the turmoil this morning? I saw a woman patting the back of a guard. He let his arms sink, he relaxed, he stepped back. I want to remember this."

"I understand," she said simply.

Later a woman guard began to read names. Everyone whose name was read was to report at the door. There were names and names and names. I had never heard so many names in my life. Then my name was read. It was like a wonderful surprise. Suddenly I felt different. I was a person again with a private life, with a past, with a future. It was exhilarating. Michelle's name was read. Her face beamed and she jumped up and hugged me and then hugged all the women around us.

"Let's go," she said, trying to pull me with her.

"No, wait, wait," I said, "I have to pack first."

"Oh, our luggage, I quite forgot." We reached for our toothbrushes and toothpaste then ran to the door.

> Michelle reminds me of my sister Elmira, who was protective of me too. When we were small she provided physical closeness I hungered for and which my parents could not give. When I think back to the time we grew up, I'm aware of invisible currents of emotions flowing between us. The spoken words were tiny marks, totally inadequate to express the complexity of those streams.
>
> But I was more like my brother in the way I

experienced the world. While my sister loved to run around with other kids, he and I more and more often preferred books for our companions.

Later he and I communicated very little with each other. Once I took a portrait painting class. Suddenly he was in my mind and I tried to conjure up his features.

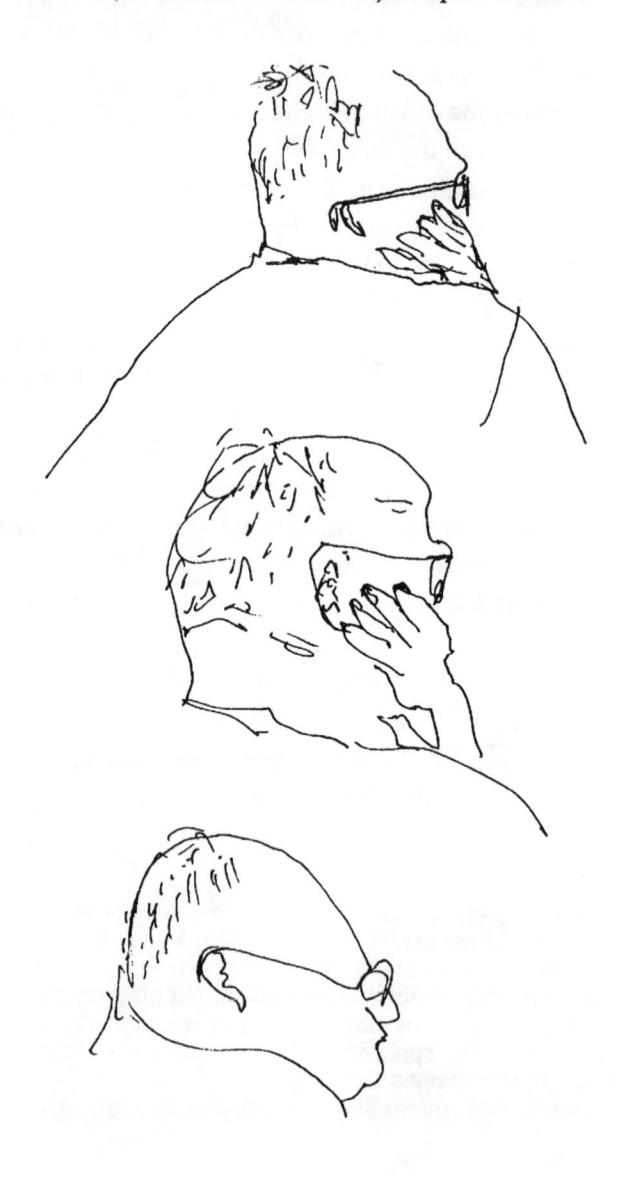

Painting My Brother's Face

MUSIC BY VIVALDI filled the studio, creating transparent patterns, garlands that swept up and down in measured joy.

The door to the outside was open, letting in an uncertain sunlight. Voices, of other students, of the instructor, entered from the adjacent room. A self-portrait of the teacher was hanging on the wall behind me. I had looked at it for a long time before turning my back, and I was still feeling its presence.

I dipped my brush into a warm orange color. I was working on a sketch of my brother's face. I painted what I sensed was hidden under his skin, a map of his emotions. It looked like a mask, one that discloses.

The sketch was not right. Only the orange glow around his chin, his lips, was true. I couldn't remember what the rest of his face expressed. I began another sketch, hoping that the brush would lead me; maybe this time an accidental line would bring it back. But there was nothing, only a black shadow that asked to be painted.

We are children again. He is standing nude on the window sill trying to shock our neighbor who is passing by—the neighbor who never smiles nor talks to us but sells us socks with drab and ugly colors. My brother is standing there holding on to the window handle and the curtains. He twists his body and squeezes his bottom against the window pane.

I remember how easily we played together, weaving in and out of each other as though we were spirits.

Please, show me your face.

And then my mother closed the bedroom doors. No more

visiting each other at bedtime. I still had a sister to snuggle, but no more funny boy's body under my covers. He was separated in order to become a man. He had to learn that brothers don't touch sisters, that lovers don't show emotions, that husbands don't relinquish space, and so many more rules like those. A shadow appeared on his forehead. It grew, and soon it resembled a black cap which he pulled down a little deeper every year.

Please, look at me just once.

The last time we met he was sitting at his executive's desk, his eyes hidden behind his thick glasses. When he turned toward me, his glance stopped before it reached me. Didn't he remember any of the games we used to play? There was still a warm glow around his mouth.

The music was gliding through my body, soothing all the cells that were in disarray, synchronizing all the rhythms that were out of phase, all the while asking me to join its slow dance, its quiet celebration.

The painting behind me was radiating warmth. I heard the instructor talking, his speech quick and precise and his thoughts shooting out of his head in flashing, vibrating silver lines. The sounds of his voice were like an embrace hovering around me, not too close, allowing me the space I needed. Several days ago those sounds had touched me and had transformed cool layers of my numbness into clouds of pulsating crimson.

I turned to look at his self-portrait. Red colors came crashing towards me like an abundance of love. An electric storm around his head. The face open, the eyes looking. A brother.

I turned back to the shaded face I was working on. "I know you are just pretending," I said. "Deep down you must remember the joy and the zest we once had."

The music rested. I heard a siren. The outside world entered with shrieks. A movie came to mind. Shooting. Wounded soldiers. Guerrillas moving through the jungle of El Salvador. Two women in the group of men, their rifles bouncing on their backs. I wondered if they had changed the rules? Were men and women merging and separating in new ways? And the day before at the pottery studio my gay friend said while wedging her clay, "The new trend is that lesbians go back to men." Suddenly I understood. They, too, are searching for their lost brothers.

I reached for the tube of white paint. I wanted to lighten the shadow on my brother's face.

The music began again, marching in graceful patterns as though trusting in a universe that was sheltering and whole.

> Dusk. The soft thud of my steps on the narrow road. Orange sky above the distant highway. Silhouettes of wintry trees.
> I'm thinking about my art class and the drawings of "White Noise" the teacher showed us. All those precise ink lines on the paper going somewhere, expressing something. They let me see the sounds. Perhaps it was the gurgle of a stream or the rustling of a tree.
> The muffled din of the traffic is woven into the roof tops and fences, the oak trees and telephone poles, the parked cars and glittering mailboxes.
> I remember so many cold evenings. Hurrying home, my feelings wound up into a tight ball. Hurrying toward a warm fire, glowing faces. Belonging.
> The lights of a car are shining at me. If it does not veer I will have to jump across the ditch. It veers and passes me.
> Cracks in the asphalt, a web of cracks. "Fractals."
> In art class the teacher talked about "fractals," a new concept to me. I'm still excited about it. Mathematicians have finally found formulas for the patterns that occur in nature. Are we coming a little closer to the blueprint of creation?
> I study the cracks in the asphalt. Lines searching eagerly. Turning right. Turning left. Getting tired. Fading. Gone.

A truck is turning into a driveway. A dog darts out, barking and jumping around. The headlights hit his wagging tail, now they light up his ears.

Puddles. Orange puddles with black trees in them.

An oak tree. The pattern of its bark is forceful, not drowsy like the asphalt's. Rectangles repeat themselves diligently, each one a little different but none forgetting its dim purpose.

Clouds in the sky; a new pattern; trying so playfully. Trying what?

All around me there is a searching, a stirring as in sleep. There is a longing to wake up, a yearning toward forms that receive, that hold and contain.

I was in a time of discovery in those days, and my art classes helped me focus. I felt tension, but not because I wanted to become an artist. I was trying to reach that rare moment when I could say, "Yes, that's right. Those lines speak to me." For that to happen I had to unlearn a great deal. I had to stop listening to my mind that continually fed me preconceived ideas. I had to become humble and begin to trust another part of myself. It was difficult to push away those layers of accumulated assumptions that concealed the real image. Those hours in the studio may have resembled exhausting therapy sessions or an arduous apprenticeship in a Zen monastery.

A Study in Light and Shadow

I CLIPPED MY DRAWING PAPER to the easel and arranged pencils and charcoal.

The fluorescent light was hammering down on me, stamping out two-dimensional shapes: human bodies, furniture, walls.

I heard easels screeching on the cement floor, paper rustling, voices—all accompanied by the blowing of the air conditioner.

A young woman took off her gown, revealing her nude body. She climbed on the podium, leaned against the wall with one hand on her hip, the other behind her neck.

"This is a twenty-minute light and shadow study. Use your paints. Forget the details." The enthusiasm in the instructor's voice made me look forward to my task.

The ceiling light was turned off, and suddenly the room was dark. A brown glow enveloped us and changed the way we were relating. Eyes and intellect had lost their importance, and there was an invitation to hush, to listen, and intuit.

I looked toward the podium. What I saw was a dazzling spectacle of lights and shadows. The model stood in the spotlights. A brilliant white blaze radiated from her shoulder and from her knee, and it ran down her leg. There was deep darkness under her arms. Reflected light played over her back, fading in and out softly and sensuously caressing it.

I squeezed some white and some dark brown paint out of the tubes and went to work.

The instructor wound his way around the easels, pointing out an inaccuracy here and there, helping us let go of prejudices and warped perceptions. Healing.

I became engrossed in my painting and stopped noticing

what was going on around me.

"Two more minutes to finish. Last checks."

I stepped back. The white and brown splashes on my paper had indeed turned into a human figure, and it looked festive and joyful to me.

"End of pose. You have a long break now."

I went outdoors, out into that blue space. My body seemed to absorb openness and sun as though it had craved them a long time.

Explosions of light were on the windshields and the chrome of the parked cars. Students were leaning against the wall and sitting on the fenders. A whiff of cigarette smoke, the crunching of a carrot. Nobody was saying much.

I saw my daughter Beryl coming across the parking lot. The sunlight dissolved her outline, and she seemed to merge with all the brightness.

"Hi, Mom." As she handed me the car keys, I could not help thinking of the party the two of us had been invited to last night. The memory moved like a dark cloud over the radiant morning. Beryl had shown me Pedro, the refugee who had killed dozens and dozens of people, who had stood eye to eye with defenseless men and women, with children, had seen their terror and pain—then shattered their bodies.

He walks across the redwood deck. A stocky Latin, shy, looks like thirty but I know he is twenty-two. I cannot read his face. A voice inside of me says, "Horrible monster." Behind him stands my daughter's English teacher, who was in Vietnam, fighting, killing. Her favorite teacher.

"But Mom," my daughter protested to me, "but Mom, Pedro was only seventeen when they forced him into the Death Squad... but Mom, if he had not killed they would have shot him... in his place I would have killed, too... Mom, I would not want to die..."

A clear straight line at the base of the page to build on. No pretense. No illusion. I saw in her a generation that accepted shadows just as much as light. I felt her strength.

Our break was over. We went back into the studio to draw- to heal ourselves, to heal the world.

    Beside me is my box of colored pencils. It's the same brand I owned when I was a child. My sister had another kind. I can hear her saying to me, "You put the purple and the green in the wrong place. You cannot borrow my pencils anymore if you make such a mess in my box." She arranges her colors according to the spectrum of the rainbow. I color diligently, but timidly, with faint lines. I did not dare to express my inner landscape, my ocean of feelings. Already I had learned to be afraid of self-expression and didn't know how to splash colors on boldly. That was not acceptable then.

    When I pick up my pencils and brushes now to capture that colorful inner world, it recedes. It doesn't want to be recognized. It leaves me, and I am sad. I have to rely on the visions of other people who are able to catch them and throw them on the canvas.

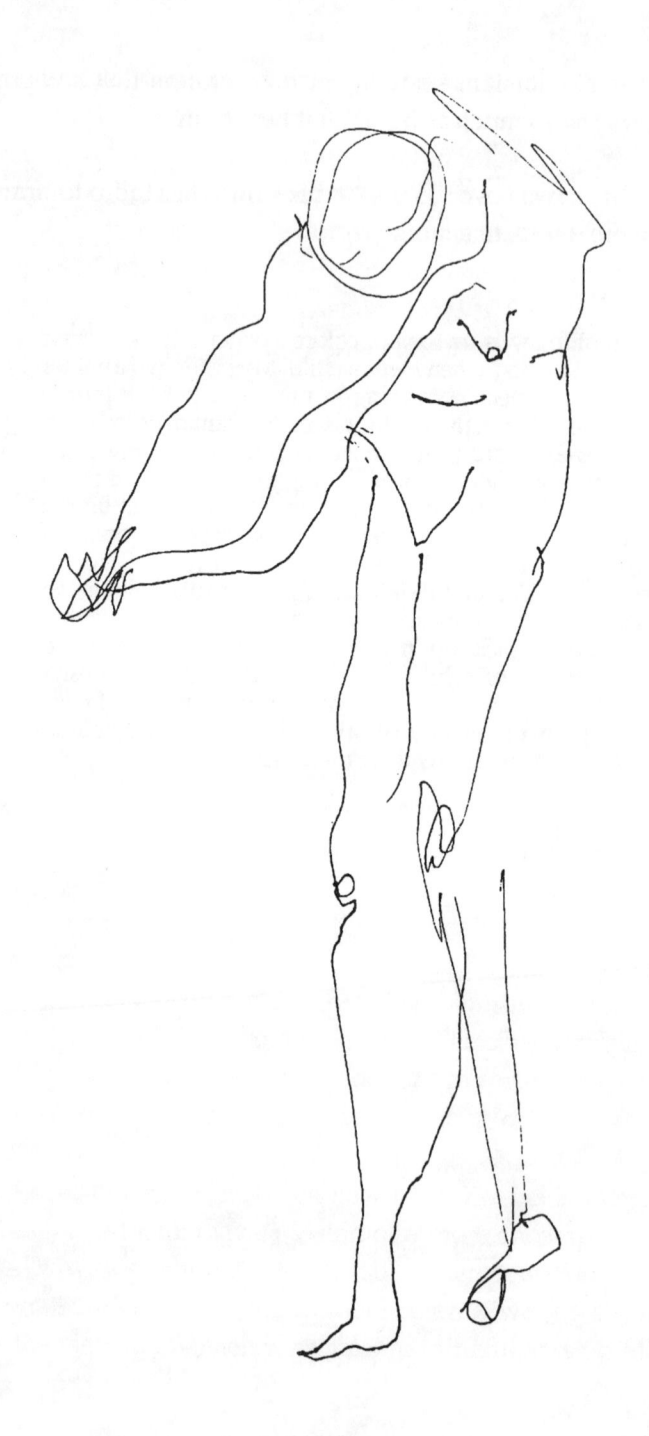

A Tour Through an Exhibit

I'M SITTING IN FRONT OF MY WINDOW with my tape recorder and my typewriter before me. I press the play button of my cassette player. The static is loud, and I have a hard time making out the words. They are about art. Sometimes the voices seem to drown in the rushing sound, sometimes they emerge clear and loud. I taped this while on a tour through the artist's house and studio.

Perhaps before I begin transcribing I should talk about Paul, the artist, and the three other women who were on the tour. But no, I won't go on describing them. It will distract from what is important to say about the exhibit.

The five of us were standing in the kitchen where the tour began. Sometimes one of us asked a question, but it usually drowned in the static. I forgot to mention that while I'm writing this down, I turn the tape recorder on and off and sometimes rewind the tape or press the fast-forward button.

My intention is to transcribe sections that are especially relevant to me to help me remember what we were looking at. By observing my reactions to the works of art, I hope to gain a better understanding of myself. The paintings will serve as mirrors to confront my own mind.

I press the play button. The voice of Paul, the artist and tour guide, surfaces. He says,

> *I use my work to become whole, to complete myself. It's like an onion with another and another layer. It's a continuous process. Ever since I was five years old I had pleasure in inviting people in. I remember a birthday party when I invited all the children of the block. I need to do this, to share my work with you. But it is not a one-way street: your presence allows me to complete myself.*

I press the stop button. Already I'm in a dilemma. This stuff is too rich and important to interrupt with my comments. I wonder what Paul means with "to complete myself." How does he achieve it? I press the play button and let the artist continue. He is talking now about "flaws."

I was working on a large painting on plywood. There was a slight depression in the board which you couldn't always see. During those months I was working on the painting I tried to ignore the depression. Every time I would recognize its presence I'd get this sinking feeling in my stomach. Finally, instead of trying to wish it away, or hide it or destroy the painting, I decided to let it guide me. So I announced it. I painted the depression with a color that was in the painting. When I did, the painting immediately was complete. "Announcing the flaw" became a philosophy for me and a liberation. I take that same focus to teaching and living.

STOP. I have to ponder about all this for a while before I can respond to it.

A thread hangs loose from the cuff of my sweat shirt. I play with it. I roll it up into a ball and then watch it unwind. I feel and rub my blisters. Now I know what to do! I'll skip the rest of the introduction the artist gave us and begin with the tour.

We looked at the masks on the kitchen wall. They were made by Paul and his family and friends. Some originated in other cultures.

Great, I thought. This was not going to be just showing off this artist; this was going to be a celebration of the creative process, and we were all included. It gave me a good feeling, and I knew we were all buoyed by it.

We left the kitchen and returned two hours later. By then the tour was over. While we were sitting at the table having lunch together, a question was asked which I now realize was the underlying theme of the tour. Audry's search for another reality prompted her question.

"Do you believe in reincarnation?"

I thought, yes, I do, but in a different way.

Paul said, "I have a hard time swallowing it."

Could I put into words quickly enough the images her question had brought up inside me and form a reply?

The new physics notion that time does not exist. A future, present and past all telescoped into each other; different realities stacked behind each other endlessly. The cartoon with the physics professor popped up in my mind:

"Ladies and gentlemen! Time was invented so that everything would not happen at the same time."

And people—like a swarming ant hill—migrating constantly, not back and forth in time, but sideways to other existences. Some move to adjacent realities; others are transported far away.

When I drifted back to the conversation, it had taken a different turn, and I took a helping of food to anchor me better in this reality.

I want to go back to the beginning of the tour. We five went from the kitchen to the hallway. There was a drinking glass with colored liquid in it. It was a picture in which Paul had faithfully painted the reflections of all the objects that were in the vicinity of the glass, though they were not visible on the canvas.

It's super-realistic but bizarre, Paul's voice breathed.

The paintings of my schizophrenic friend Olaf come to my mind.

There is really nothing in common with his pictures and

Paul's glass except the brilliant colors and the fact that Olaf draws the reflection of something I cannot see. He is always making those strange patterns of lines, like some kind of energy flow. It looks broken up, but nonetheless there is order and beauty in it, and when I look at Olaf's pictures they make me feel good. I think of him often these days. I imagine him hanging around door frames a lot when he was growing up, not wanting to join, not wanting to go far away.

We left the hallway and entered another room. There was a painting of the head of a woman. It was awkward and powerful at the same time. Richard, a mentally handicapped man we both knew, had painted it in Paul's art class.

It's honest, you can't belittle it, the voice on the tape says.

A memory crosses my mind.

I knock at a tiny house with weeds growing happily around it. Richard opens the door. He is tall; his posture is slightly asymmetric. He lets me step in. His body seems to curve away from me, creating an open space while his head with red hair and freckles is listening intensely to something far away that I cannot hear. Shall I address the powerful child in him or the thin layer of adult male that covers him?

Later during the tour, Paul showed us the portrait he had painted of Richard showing a double image of him and the mysterious connection he had with sounds coming from another dimension. Paul had boldly represented Richard's hearing of inaudible vibrations that I had vaguely intuited.

We four women and Paul, grouped around a large painting. It was of a section of a forest, vibrating with colors. Paul is talking.

It's behind our house where we used to live. I could only work 10 or 20 minutes at a time—the light—all the shapes—it was overwhelming. It took me three days to put it on the canvas... then I experimented with the colors; there was an army of greens; I mixed one color after the other until I had it right...it took me three weeks... It was a spiritual kind of concentration... If you rock back and forth a little it becomes three-dimensional. (Little chirps of surprise from us.)—Yes, that's true.

I press the STOP button.

※

I haven't worked on this story for a long time.

Today the slant of the winter sun hits my table, warms up the metal of my typewriter and makes me pull off my sweatshirt.

Perhaps I had pressed those forward and rewind buttons too fast, so suddenly the tape jammed, and I couldn't eject it anymore. I sent the machine to the manufacturer. I received it back a few weeks later. When I pressed the eject button, the compartment opened. It was empty. No tape. I was appalled. I had lost the artist's words, his voice, the music he had composed and the whole material for my story. It was a bad moment.

Gradually I noticed a feeling of relief. I was free, no longer did I have to painstakingly pry out the words from the static and worry that I misunderstood or misinterpreted them. I thought about Paul welcoming flaws and the liberation it can bring.

In my mind I saw the factory where they had worked on my recorder.

The technician who fixes my machine, out of sheer boredom is pulling the whole tape off its spools and dropping it on the floor. It cascades down in soft swirls and the linear tyranny of those 120 minutes is now broken. Time goes backward and forward, crosses and loops over itself, twists and turns and is transformed into a delicate sculpture.

Even if the technician was curious and had listened to the whole tape he could not have eavesdropped to the last part of the tour. It was not recorded. By the time we arrived at the artist's studio—which felt like a kiva to me—the tape had come to an end without my noticing it. The magic that happened there couldn't have been recorded by a machine anyhow.

I remember the last sentences on the lost tape spoken just before we entered the studio. They were about the canoe man, a figure the artist knew from his dreams. Paul was still working on him, and I wondered what kind of boat he would build for the figure. I thought it could be very delicate because dreamers and the dead who cross over to that other world have no weight. I was touched that Paul had materialized a thought that had recently surfaced in my mind now and again.

From now on I have to recall the tour without the help of the tape. I left off when we were gathering around a painting called the forest. When I saw this work a few years ago, I barely looked at it and walked away. I had felt like fleeing. This time I stopped with the group and made an effort to look. I saw a jungle teeming with life, an abundance of details that overwhelmed and confused me. Gazing at this painting again I realized that it couldn't swallow me up, that I was safe. Still, I felt a longing for distance and the quietness of clear, simple shapes that could be isolated from each other, named and understood. I will remember, I thought, that I don't have to flee from the chaotic side of life.

After standing there awhile, we discovered all sorts of unintended little pictures in it. Faces, animals, the head of a horse; all appeared, and disappeared again.

Paul said that he was fascinated with that moment when one image falls apart and becomes another in the viewer's mind.

It's a magic moment, I know. It puts a question mark by everything you see. It's a trick to lure another dimension into this reality.

❋

I'm sitting on the deck wondering when I will ever finish this story. Am I stuck like my tape was before? What is the hurdle I have to get over? The tour was at the beginning of winter, and now I'm enjoying the first signs of spring. The coyote bush across from me is letting go of its parachutes, and the wind makes the seed twirl across the planks. A wisp of the winter coat of my cat joins in, and now all those white fuzzy things dance around together. What a perfect scene for a Japanese haiku!

I won't even try to write one. To compose the last line of the little poem, you almost need an oriental mind. They treat their poetry like a soap bubble: They make you see it, then they pop it, and finally they show you the ring of foam that marks its former outline. It's not a question of which is more valid, the big bubble or the little foam. What counts is the "pop," that little jolt in our mind that tells us how we create reality. We produce images so quickly and slap them on a background so closely together that we think that's all there is. It's only when a picture pops, or when the next one is delayed, that we sometimes become aware of the slim white edges between them and understand that the white background underneath is the deeper reality.

For some people, the edges are so wide that they cannot handle it. My friend Olaf holds on tightly to his scattered images, but they are too far apart and don't allow him to get a footing in our customary reality.

I'm back at my desk. There is a cobweb in the corner of my window. A brown spider is hanging inside, upside down. My breath makes web and creature rock gently.

I remember Paul saying, "I never enjoyed writing." We were looking at a painting called *Confessions of an Outsider*. It had letters on it that were partially blocked out by an invisible grid.

"Writing is difficult for a left-hander," the artist explained. "Sometimes I had to stay after school."

"School, letters, writing…" I muse.

I paint capitals five inches high. They all have personality. I like the R with its stiff, pretentious gait. But my favorite is the S, the mysterious stranger, that has joined the alphabet. This outsider and I share a secret.

Now we are bigger. I practice handwriting, squeezing letters between tight lines. The teacher looks over my shoulders. The fabric of his black suit is shiny with age. The toes of his boots are bent upwards. Once in a P.E. class he not only takes off his jacket but also opens his vest. I can see that a starched collar and a starched breast are attached to his undershirt, its long sleeves are held back by elastics. I go home and tell my mother about the fragmented fashion of his clothes. She breaks out in her clear, silvery laugh.

A swing hits the teacher's head. He is in pain. He slaps the boy who did it; the kid almost topples over. I'm not surprised that the pious man lost his temper, but I am amazed that he feels pain. He actually feels pain!

Now he takes my paper, and with dismay in his voice he says, "This is not good enough; you have to try harder." But I try so hard already. I'm crushed.

My mind wanders back to Paul's letters on the canvas. They are short limbed and undeveloped as though he had sent them back to babyhood. He had pushed them to a place that lies to the left in the geography of my inner world. He had explored that region when he painted "The Forest," and when he drew "White Noise" pictures. I know what happens when you go farther and farther to the left. You arrive at the place where all things emerge, where you can hear the speechless hum of creation.

I feel much more comfortable at the right, and I want to push my marks in that direction of the cycle. It's at the right, near the edge of reality, where I feel at home. There I would like to tip my creations over so that they could float out into a medium where meaning can exist by itself without the need for form and matter.

Gradually a vague idea begins forming in my mind about wholeness and what it might mean to me. Those paintings coax me to try new experiences.

I remember, at some point our group climbed to the second story. At the top of the stairs Paul pointed out a painting in red and blue done by a former high school student of his, his name was Dylan. I took one quick glance at the picture then averted my eyes. I don't want to deal with this raw emotion, I thought. At once I forgot about it.

A few weeks after the tour, Paul came into the classroom and told me that Dylan, the young man whose painting we had seen, had committed suicide. I could only remember a red and blue painting at the top of the staircase and that I had averted my eyes. If I had met Dylan in person I might have shunned him the same way. Today I think I did not want to acknowledge those uncomfortable red and blue feelings in myself, so I looked away when I passed his painting.

When Paul told us, I was unpacking art materials. I had brought some black surfaces because I wanted to draw white lines, reversing the usual black marks on white. Paul said he just came from the burial, and in spite of the sadness there was a feeling of liberation. I said I understood what he meant. A memory came back...

She is telling us of her dream of elephants breaking into her backyard. From then on we take turns staying at her bedside, watching her. It's the afternoon of the night when she will die. I sit near her bed listening to the rattling sound of her breath. Outside the wind is blowing furiously. Two days ago she had become alert again and had asked us for a cup of Earl Gray tea. We scurried into the kitchen, filled with the insane hope she would recover, at least for a while. Unconcerned for the subtle aroma of her favorite tea, one friend dissolved a spoonful of honey in the tea to give her energy, another one dripped some lemon juice into it. Out of fear of death we ruined the last treat life had to offer her. She took one sip, smiled, and fell back into her pillows.

Outside a fierce wind is blowing. The rattle of the breath goes on and on. Suddenly, it occurs to me: but this is a birth! And when I go home, I feel the excitement in the air, the feeling of freedom that soothes my pain and anguish.

I can hear Olaf quoting his aunt, "'Olaf, you are not alive. You are not dead.'" And he repeats her words with a mixture of pain and amusement. "She said to me, 'You are not alive, and you are not dead.'"

Olaf has been trying to push his way into the story for awhile. It is time to let him come in.

A knock at the door. He steps in, tall, athletic.

"Can I talk to you?"

He settles in a chair and stares at the floor in silence. His hands rest on his thighs. In the warm light of the lamp his hands are very beautiful, except there is a newness about them as though they were kept in a jewelry box for a long time without being used.

Now he raises his head and looks at me. I almost feel his glance tap my forehead. After a second or two he takes a deep breath and begins to talk.

I wonder about these glances that shoot out of his gray eyes. Sometimes I get the feeling that he is compressed between two walls, the one in front of him so high that he can barely see above it. Other times it appears that he is standing in water up to his nose, his eyes saying half in jest, "Here I am, come find me!"

His glance does something to me. It is as though an anchor were dropped inside of me, and I feel it settling heavily into my ground.

He is clear, articulate and talks in a gentle way. I wander with him along the narrow street of his existence. There seem to be houses, and trees, and cars, as in the regular world. But when I look behind them, there is nothing there. They are like theater props, two-dimensional. I have an eerie feeling. Beyond this thin slice of reality, terror looms.

"Sometimes I feel like hitting my fist against the wall. I won't do it because it makes me crazy, but sometimes it takes all my energy to keep myself calm."

He takes a deep breath as though to lift the sigh that is frozen in his chest, then goes on.

"I don't take notice of necessary things. I'm a little confused, things like old towels, paper tissues that have to be taken care of. I don't know what I expect of myself. If we go out for coffee I don't know, is this all I can have or should I buy some more?"

I want to call out to him, "Stop, stop, go back to your bedroom and your thought about things on the floor, you were not finished, take a stand!"

I don't, and he slides on to the next incident in that uncanny transition where his self extinguishes and in a moment reappears. He—unable to experience the continuity of his self—relies on echoes and reflections cast by his presence to tell him that he is.

From my perspective all his selves are one, and in place of his ego that never formed I say to him, "Indeed, you are."

He replies with a grateful smile. "That's all I have to say tonight." Getting up he asks, "May I give you a hug?"

He stoops. He seems to wrap air around me, and the tender grasp of his fingers awakens a silvery image of a child of mine returning.

It's very quiet. Sometimes I can hear a little sound in the walls from the cracking of wood. It's dark outside, and in the window pane I can only see the reflection of the typewriter, the lamp and myself. I look at this person across from me that seems to be outdoors and is not clearly visible. There appears to be another part of myself out there that is mysterious, unexplored, elusive.

There is not much to tell anymore. We came to the end of the tour. We passed the canoe man and entered the kiva-like wooden structure. On one level everything was ordinary. The painting, "West," dominated the room. We walked around, looked at the portrait of Richard, listened to Paul's music, admired this and that while my tape machine was humming but not recording. We sat down in chairs, and the artist told us a dream and acted it out. And then at some moment we passed through the white edge.

Our bodies become fragile, layers and layers peel off. With our thoughts hushed and with our soles treading over the soft soil of the dream country we follow the artist towards West, its mountains and forests still forming and becoming. We are on an island in a river. Its water, our concept of time, is rushing by and does not affect us. The island turns into a boat. Paul is in front, we are behind. We all belong together with one skin enfolding us all. The boat goes uphill as though on a mountain of water, up, up.

We were back in the kitchen. We sat around the table and talked. One woman asked, "Do you believe in reincarnation?" Or did she say, "Is it true that we just migrated together into an adjacent reality?"

I answer her, "Yes, it is true. We are still in it. That's why we feel more complete than before."

She nods. "I think I understand."

> The visit to the art show infused me with creative energy that not only expressed itself in my own drawing and painting but spilled over into my entire daily routine. Often I had to leave my art class early and go to my part-time jobs. I was a counselor in a home for schizophrenic people. At my other job I was teaching mentally handicapped people as I had done thirty years earlier. This time my students were adults.
>
> Sometimes I felt that drawing was work, hard inner work, while my paying job was like attending a class where I had to listen and observe. But whether drawing bodies or studying my client's behavior, both satisfied my need to explore human beings. I tried to keep myself open and alert like a photographer with a camera to capture whatever touched me in the other person. Sometimes it was just a small gesture like being given a bit of paper for a present.

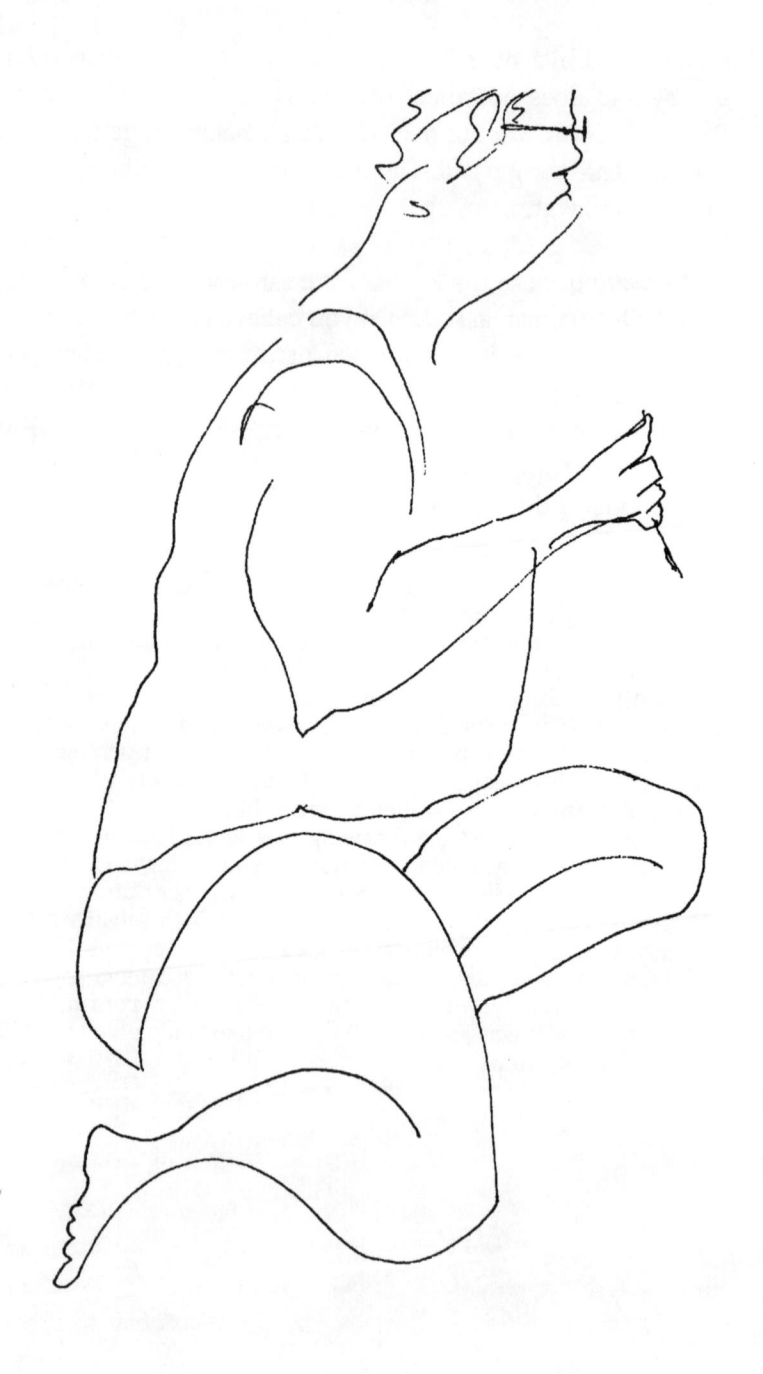

The Bus Ticket

I WAS SUPERVISING DURING LUNCH BREAK at a workshop for developmentally disabled adults. There was an earthiness in the room that made me feel grounded. Was it because the hall used to be a barn with troughs that were now converted into long tables; was it because of the inarticulate sounds I was hearing; or was it something else?

The men and women who were only mildly retarded had been working in the plant nursery this morning. Some were now sitting or lying on one of the tables, listening to country music from a portable radio. Others were sitting on chairs, eating their sandwiches.

The severely retarded people were grouped together at another table. Among them were five women with Down's syndrome who now, one after another, closed their lunch boxes, left their eating place and sat down on couches that were arranged in a square. Shelly, an older woman with white hair, followed them. Debbie and Susan were left at the table.

The five laughed and giggled. I had tried to follow their conversation and find out what made them laugh, but they had their secret cues which I didn't understand. Now I just listened to their sounds, especially Bonnie's. She was obese. Her giggles went up and down the scale. In between laughter she let her thick tongue drop on her chin, while eyes full of mischief glanced over the rim of her glasses. I had seen her dancing the other day; she moved like a feather in spite of her weight.

Then I noticed that the laughing had stopped. Mary was crying—with her double chin and the profile of an Austrian empress. Her neighbor put an arm around her and drew her closer. Mary let her head drop on her friend's chest. Another friend got up and threw a candy into Mary's lap. She stuffed it into her pocket. Her eyelids were red from crying. Cheryl from the other group approached and said,

"Don't cry. Go wash your face, you will feel better. Go wash your face, go now."

But Mary was comfortable where she was. A few more sobs then she was happy again, her eyes clear and sparkling.

Donald was walking up and down between the tables. He was in his fifties, six feet tall, haggard, his face ravaged with his sickness (schizophrenia they said) and its treatment. The left corner of his mouth hung down; the left eye was more closed and seemed lower than the other. Ever so often there was a hesitation in his gait. Just when I thought he was going out the door, he turned around. I had to watch him so he wouldn't fill his pockets with all kinds of things or smoke a cigarette somewhere and cause a fire.

Once when I asked him to draw something, he painted a yellow square on his paper and said, "This is my pillow." Then he went on decorating it with blue flowers. I liked him. There was a gentleness in his face and a sensitivity hidden under his wild looks.

Charles had been standing near Donald's path for a while. He had Down's syndrome like the five women. Compared to Donald, he was a dwarf with a bulging stomach. His chin protruded. He was toothless and had the habit of pushing his lower jaw forward and backward in a grotesque way.

Now Donald was approaching and Charles stretched out his chubby hand. Donald stopped, shook hands. A short smile relaxed his mouth, then he continued his restless wandering. Charles smacked his lips, threw his head back and returned to his chair.

Debbie rose stiffly from her seat at the table.

"Are you finished with your lunch?" I asked.

"Ye-e-e-s, fi-ni-shed." Her voice dragged and sounded like

a creaking door that was opened slowly. Her rigid, pencil-like figure almost leaned backward when she walked. She threw a crumpled paper in the garbage, then stopped in her movement. She leaned over, staring into the trash can. Staring. Finally she unbent and walked back to her chair. Her arm was up and her fingers near her face seemed to flick something off her thumb, as though she was trying forever to get rid of some trifle or some unpleasant thought. I felt fear when I first saw her; her woodenness seemed inhuman. One day I put my hand on her shoulder. She turned around, and I saw that her face was alive.

Susan's timer rang. I went over to her and handed her an M&M candy. It was her reward for being good for the last twenty minutes, for not screaming and cursing. She put the candy in her mouth quickly, closed her lunch pail, got up and followed Danny, her boyfriend, to the couch. Susan was beautiful. I never got tired of looking at her rich auburn hair, her pale face with her eyes embedded in softness. She had had one of her outbursts this morning and had filled the house with her screams and her "fuck you, fuck you, fuck you." When she was in my classroom afterwards, she blamed herself. She mumbled,

"I blew it today, I sure blew it. I was bad, I blew it." She seemed to replay a tape of all the voices that had tried to make her adjust.

I told her that she was okay, that I liked her. But could she hear me?

Both she and Danny were twenty-two or twenty-three. He was a friendly guy, and there was something wholesome about him. They wrapped their arms around each other and pressed cheek against cheek. We had been asked not to tolerate close physical contact between the clients. Only handholding was permitted.

I wondered what the time limit of a kiss was in a PG rated

movie? I set it arbitrarily for ten seconds and watched the time. Ten seconds were over and they were still glued together. I felt touched by the purity and innocence of their gesture and did not interfere.

Someone flopped down in a corner. It was Donald who finally had stopped marching, and curled up as though the cement floor were a cozy bed. Debbie was the only one of her group who was still sitting at the table. She was still flicking her fingers, oblivious to the rest of the world.

Susan and Danny's heads were now apart and he spoke softly to her.

Shelly tried to open a can. I could see the frustration in her face. She couldn't pull off the tab. She had been anxious and tense all morning. I watched her closely. She was probably my age. If she were living in my reality I would choose her for a friend. We would sit together, drink tea and talk for a long time. She struck me as a person who could tune in and listen patiently, an attentive smile on her face.

I saw her anxiety mounting. I could have gone over to her and opened her drink, or better, touched her, said a kind word, and her frustration might have disappeared. The psychologist thought we should not do that. Shelly should learn to ask for help if she needed it. She had to find her own support, had to become self-reliant. One day—at least in theory—she might go out into a world that did not always lend a helping hand. She had to be toughened for a tough life.

I felt she was only seconds away from an outbreak. My own tension increased. I got up to be closer to her. If she started screaming I would have to lead her to a separate small room. There was nothing in it except a heavy table and a chair. If she threw the chair against the wall I would have to take it away from her. I had to leave her alone with the door open so that she could get out if she wanted to.

Her throwing and kicking hadn't disturbed me very much

when it had happened before. It was her screams that tore me apart. Those forlorn shrieks that fell into my heart like stones. Her spirit was imprisoned, and the open door didn't help. She revolted against a world that didn't love her, that didn't love her enough to set her free. I knew she was right. And Susan and Debbie were right when they screamed and howled out their pain, trying to cut holes through the viscosity of our indifference. I was part of that world they were accusing.

A hand reached over to Shelly, took her can. Danny opened it and gave it back to her. Her pained expression left. She looked at him intensely, with gratitude. I felt thankful, too.

Now, a short, chubby fellow walked into the room. Fred, too, had Down's syndrome. He was an American Indian with olive skin and short gray hair that stuck out like bristles. He saw me and dragged a chair toward me. The screech of its legs on the cement floor hurt my ears. He pushed his chair right against mine. His purposefulness was disarming.

Fred had a strange face, flat, with big eye sockets. When I saw his profile, his forehead and chin protruded more than his nose. If I saw a friendly creature like him in the forest what would I name him? I wondered. He sat down as close to me as he could. Instead of using his rudimentary speech he made two low grunts. He gently grabbed my wrist and put my hand on his head. He wanted me to feel his new haircut. I had expected his hair to feel prickly, but instead it was soft like a freshly mowed lawn. I told him that. He began to smile. His smile grew over his face. His eyes widened. There was utter trust and openness in them. A light was radiating from him as though from another world. It made my body melt and my mind become humble.

He reached into his shirt pocket and gave me a used bus ticket, indicating that I should keep it. I felt tears coming to my eyes.

It was almost one o'clock and time for him to go back to his classroom. He would learn how to count to ten and how to sort colored pegs. I felt that perhaps in some way Fred was the real teacher, and that he was not retarded but ahead of all of us on the road toward perfect love.

Each time I walked toward the workshop to teach the handicapped persons, my mood shifted back and forth from the anticipation of the enormous amount of energy and patience I had to put in to change the behavior of my clients, to the hope of being rewarded with a small sign of response that made my work worthwhile.

Later I didn't work with groups anymore but with individuals who had been moved out of care homes. Each one now lived by himself or herself in an apartment. I was hired to go there and teach them the necessary skills to live independently.

Raymond

I WAS DRIVING THROUGH TOWN when I saw Raymond. I recognized him from far away because of his shuffling gait and red hair. He was gesticulating and talking to himself.

My first impulse was to drive by. It wasn't class time, and it was not part of my job to deal with his problems in my free time. But I stopped anyhow. He walked toward me, his body softly padded like a baby's, his belly protruding. His spine had lost its flexibility and made him look old. Guessing his age was impossible. He had one shirttail tucked in, one out. His pants were riding precariously below his waist. I rolled down the car window.

"Hi, Raymond, what's the matter? Why are you upset?" He came over to me. He was talking so excitedly that I couldn't understand what he was saying. The glasses on the tip of his nose were opaque with dirt. Small blue eyes shooting in all directions. Red stubble sprouting on pink skin. He was such a mess, such a burden, I wished I could just drop him from my life.

"Jeff took my keys," he wailed in his high voice, "he won't give them back to me. How can I get in my house now?"

I clenched my teeth and said, "Come, get into my car."

His anxiety left him immediately. We drove to Jeff's, his coworker, who returned the keys which he had taken in jest. Raymond lightened up. There was a silent chuckle in his face, and I could almost see soap bubbles come out of his body. I felt quite good myself.

Later that same day I met him in a restaurant, not as his teacher but as a friend to celebrate his 28th birthday. I told myself to make the best of this; I'll ignore his unkemptness and his sluggish mind and focus on what is behind his ridiculous exterior. I'm sure I'll learn something new about him.

He sat across from me in the booth. He smiled at his hamburger. When he tried to put the two buns together, lettuce and tomato pieces spilled over the table, the tray and his lap. His coordination was so bad that it seemed as though he was doing everything in a rocking boat. He said to himself, "Raymond, you made a mess, but I'll clean it up." He put the lettuce pieces back on the plate and with his hand trembling he let the tomato pieces drop on the bun. He took the first bite, head tilted, eyes closed, and I felt that his whole awareness was inside his mouth.

"It's delicious," he mumbled while chewing. "Are you only eating a salad?" he asked in disbelief.

The problem is me, I thought. Raymond has cleaned his glasses and can see me, but my view of him is still obscured with prejudices. I don't really want to be here with him.

"Erika," Raymond said in his childlike pleading manner as though his voice wanted to snuggle up with me, "can you find Maury's address and give it to me? He moved again. He is in Oakland."

He had asked me this before but I had forgotten. Maurice, that spunky brother of his, used to be my client, too. Maurice dreamt of living in the country, taking care of farm animals. I wished I could have found him a place. In my fantasy I gave him a ranch with lots of animals to feed. Now I can see him strutting through the streets of Oakland in his boots and cowboy hat. Sometimes perhaps he hears the pigs grunt, those pigs I have created for him, and he feels a wet snout push against his hand. He still hopes he can buy a piece of land for a hundred dollars, because one hundred is the highest amount his mind can grasp. He gets cheated and exploited but he always survives.

Raymond interrupted my inner pictures.

"Barry and Tyler kissed again in the workshop. I don't do

what they do. My Mom told me to keep away from gays and from drugs." He had told me this already twenty times.

"What else did she teach you?" I asked, hoping for a statement I hadn't heard before.

He lowered his eyes and thought.

"She taught us how to cook. She said when she was dead we had to take care of ourselves. She died of cancer. I don't do what Barry and those guys are doing, kissing another man, yuk. I hug my brother Maury, but that's different. He's my kid brother, I love him. Maury lives in Oakland now."

The two brothers could perhaps live together, I thought.

"Did Lois come back?" I asked Raymond.

"No, no, she won't come back. The manager told her he would call the police. She couldn't stay another night."

"Are you glad she left?"

"Yeah," he said in a vague way.

I was a little disappointed that she had had to move out. Lois was not retarded. She was a drifter and about the age of my oldest daughter. She was an uncompromising woman who followed her wildest urges. Strange that Raymond brought her into my life when I felt weighed down with "shoulds" and "shouldn'ts" and when my dreams mirrored my feelings of being stuck in my life. In a recent dream I was going on a journey but there were no suitcases, and I had lots of stuff I wanted to take with me, so I couldn't leave. This young woman, Lois, had no belongings and had left her child in a foster home so she could be free while I, in my dream, wanted to carry even my pillows with me.

"Your brother took some people in, too, sometimes, like you did with Lois. Remember those last visitors before Maurice moved away from here?" I asked.

How well I remember those folks! I can see the black man with the crutches sitting on Maurice's beaten-up couch, watching TV. His unhealthy complexion has a shade of green in it. Handsome Carlos is singing in the shower, while a pale, silent woman stands in the kitchen, holding a child in one arm, stirring a pot with the other hand. Maurice is strutting through his home. He is proud and exhilarated because now he has friends and is important.

I had never met Melville, the black man, but in some way he was not a stranger. His expression resembled a clay mask I had made years before. Like my mask, Melville's long, severe face looked into the distance, envisioning an ideal world far away. I could see him move stiffly, painfully, leaning on his crutches because at some point his goal had lost its colors and had petrified, and he stopped traveling toward it. Ever so often his shadow limped before my inner eyes acting out a part I could choose to play in my life at any moment.

Melville had stirred me on some level, and I wondered if, in turn, Melville was moved by Maurice. What feelings welled up in this sick man when he saw a mindless kid strut through life so trustfully?

Sometimes Melville and Carlos would sit outside of Maurice's apartment and flash a gun to keep the neighbors away. The realtor wanted them out, and the agency that had hired me to teach Maurice wanted them out. Those guys! They lied and stole and threatened people and I don't know what else—but with Maurice, who accepted them unconditionally, they could let their good nature come through. I hated to tell those visitors that they had to move out.

Aloud, I said to Raymond, "They stayed in Maurice's apartment for a few weeks and managed to leave a couple of hours before the police arrived."

"Did the police find them?"

"I don't know if they even tried to. The group lived in the campground for a while, then they split up and a little later Maurice moved up north."

"Maury moved again. He lives in Oakland now."

"Your brother was glad when he had his apartment all to himself again. What will you do if Lois moves back?"

"She won't," he said quickly, "the manager will call the police on her. She is living with a boyfriend."

"I hope not with the one who wanted to run her over with his truck or the one who went after her other boyfriend with a knife," I said.

"No, her new boyfriend wouldn't do that," Raymond said.

"You damned Indian!" the words popped up in my mind. Those were the words an old man said to Lois. He was sitting on a bench in front of Safeway. She had turned to me and said,

"I may be an Indian, but I'm not damned."

Back in Raymond's trailer she began unpacking the groceries. I had looked around for a place to put down my backpack and notebook. I wondered if there were still lice living in the upholstery. The kitchen chairs were heaped high with clothes and towels. The table was covered with crumbs, drips of red jam, envelopes, bills all wrinkled and fingerprinted, a condom in its wrapper between the salt and pepper shaker, a greasy dishrag stiffened into a permanent sculpture.

Lois ran into the bedroom and returned.

"Raymond," she cried happily, "I found your suspenders. They were under the bed."

She stuffed Raymond's shirttail into his pants with rough, seemingly angry movements, then clipped the suspenders to the back of his pants. She yanked him around and attached them in front also. He let it all happen, relaxed, a tiny smile on his face.

"Raymond, you smell like old cheese," she shouted, "go take a shower!"

"Maybe tomorrow," he said lazily.

"No, you have to take a shower every day," she yelled at him.

"Okay, Mommy, I'll take one later," he said appeasingly.

"I'm not your Mommy, you jerk," she said a little milder, because his defenselessness had begun to heal the hurt she was carrying around with her, and she flopped prone on the mattress that was on the floor, extending her arms in front of her.

"Please, clean your table," I said to the Raymond who was in the trailer while Raymond who was sitting across from me in the restaurant put his hamburger down and said, "Erika, I want to ask you something." He modulated his speech so that his voice seemed to shimmer and sparkle. "Can we have a cooking class soon?" Now his voice had become almost transparent and it fluttered. The wing of a butterfly brushed against me. This wing, this voice: weightless and immaterial, it had found its way inside of me and forced me to accept this union which—for one second—lifted me out of my body and let me float, blissfully, limitlessly. "Can you show me how to make lasagna?"

"Sure," I replied, "how about tomorrow?"

"Oh, good," he said happily.

He sneezed. A blob of green mucus dangled from his nostril and attached itself to his moustache. He didn't care or didn't notice. A shiver of disgust ran through my body.

"Raymond, wipe your nose."

He took his napkin and did, then stared at what he had removed; finally he crumpled up his napkin.

This man is a foreigner in our culture, I thought. He will never adjust to our grooming and dressing habits. But wait—maybe he is a foreigner in our reality. I can see he is not quite accustomed to moving around in this world. He trembles and sways—he ignores the signposts with which we label our reality… "What year is it?" he may ask. "Is it 1978 or what?" He has difficulty distinguishing fact from fantasy. He has said so many times that Maurice moved to Oakland that it sounds like the truth. As a matter of fact I began to believe it myself. But he made it all up.

Raymond draped his arms around the plate so that his hands touched and his arms formed a circle. It was a posture of perfect contentment. I realized that he had washed his hands not because the grime disturbed him but because he wanted to please me. The skin on his hands was very white. I saw the pink ovalness of his fingernails. His fingers were tapered as though he wanted to touch the world gently. I felt they were longing to feel something soft, perhaps a rabbit fur, and wanted to bury themselves in it.

Then I could see those hands sticking, not out of a worn polyester jacket, but out of a velvet coat. They were holding a book bound in soft leather. This Raymond was much older and was standing in the library of a mansion. His eyes expressed more consciousness but they shone with the same optimism: as though they had just seen the sun rise above the horizon, and that was enough to fill them with complete trust in the universe.

Raymond in the restaurant began to talk and the other one blurred and vanished.

"I'm sorry, I can't finish. I'm full." He looked regretfully at the little piece of bread, the three or four French fries and the lettuce left on his plate. "I know it is a waste of money but I'm really full." He got up. "I think I want to walk home. Thank you for the good meal."

He shuffled out of the restaurant. I was relieved that he had left. But then I noticed that a small part of myself had shuffled out with Raymond, and for a moment that hurt.

> One of my other clients was Morna. I enjoyed going to her apartment because she loved people so much. I taught her how to cook and how to write checks. Each

time she played the same ritual to celebrate my coming.

I knock at her door. She opens it wide but hides behind it. I enter and pretend I don't know where she is and call her. She runs around me, goes outside into the hallway and closes the door behind her.

I know, out there in the hall she is anticipating the joy of hugging and greeting me, but for a little longer she wants to experience the separation. I open the door for her and she bursts in, clasping me in a tight hug. There is no sensuality in her hug nor even tenderness; rather she presses her compact body against mine like a tree would hug another tree, just being so joyous that they both exist.

Then she starts gliding down by moving her legs apart. I have to hold her up and once more she can indulge in the longed-for closeness. I tickle her neck a little; she bobs up on her toes and lets out a little scream. At last we let go, look at each other and I ask her how she is. Once more she hugs me, this time shorter, she is almost ready to separate. Then she walks away to the kitchen to prepare our meal. Her voice sounds matter-of-fact, and she begins working in a steady and efficient way.

Morna liked almost everyone; however she was a little uneasy with Barry. She seemed to be especially uncomfortable when he got teased for his homosexuality.

Barry

I SAID SOMETHING TO BARRY. We looked at each other. Suddenly his eyes became blurred and the outline of his pupil faded into the iris. There were green and brown specks in the membrane, and in each there was the small square of the reflected kitchen window. I could have called back the young man's attention easily, but I didn't want to disturb what he was experiencing in that other dimension. Maybe it was more important than what I was teaching him here.

Those eyes were set in a suntanned face which was quite good looking. I knew that face well. I had drawn it many times while waiting for him to finish a task. Without looking at my paper, my glance would follow the slant of his forehead, the sharp inside curve to the bridge of his nose, down straight to the tip; finally to his full mouth. The lower lip and the chin were receding as though fleeing action. The whole face was rather bony and cleanly molded.

In the meantime my hand had created Barry's profile or rather a caricature of it. Once, when I drew him, his features looked noble like those of a Greek god; another time they were jammed into each other, and it appeared he had withdrawn completely into himself. There was one picture I did when his lips were moving and all the lines were jumbled up, looking as if Barry was trying to untangle himself from mixed-up thoughts and confused emotions.

Barry's eyes were still directed toward me, and I began to feel embarrassed. Suddenly his pupils narrowed, their outline became sharp and life returned to his eyes. He blinked while shaking his head. "I was daydreaming again," he said.

"Were you dreaming of Tyler or of Danny?" I asked jokingly.

"Oh, I don't know. Maybe both." He pushed out a nervous laugh, "Ha, ha."

"Let's go on with your budget," I said. We sat down.

"Today is March 23rd, 1988," he said decidedly.

I watched him write. He held his pencil with so much force that the round numbers and letters became angular, and the zeros and eights looked like boxes someone had kicked around.

I felt comfortable sitting with Barry at his kitchen table. It was as if he had woven an invisible tapestry that surrounded us like a tent. It was soft and structured as a bat's wing. It held me in a gentle embrace. Each time I came to his home I let myself glide into that mellow circle. But being his teacher I sometimes wondered whether it was good to step out of my authoritative role and allow such closeness.

His supervisors at work who couldn't have this one-to-one relationship with him and who had to give him orders, experienced him as obstinate and called him a "pain in the neck." But inside that web he and I could work together like a team, and I found him easy to guide most of the time.

While Barry wrote his numbers, I opened my notebook and skimmed over the entries I had made over the last few months.

November 10: I found 7 bottles of ketchup, 4 jars of strawberry jam, 6 jars of mayonnaise in his refrigerator all opened and mostly empty.

"How is your jar collection?" I asked Barry and opened the refrigerator.

"Oh, you are just like my Mom," he said half joking, half blaming.

"It looks good in here today," I said and closed the door.

November 17: Barry said when he kissed Danny today, Tyler got jealous and pouted. Later they made up. "They both love me and look up to me," he said.

December 2: Barry got fired from his kitchen job because of his teasing. He is now working in a landscaping crew.

I said to Barry, "When I was small, my father teased me a lot. It really hurt me. I wonder why he did it."

"He was probably jealous," Barry said.

"Jealous? How do you mean?"

"I don't know."

Barry put down his pencil and folded his hands behind his head. With his elbows sticking out and his long legs spread apart his body took up the whole length of the table.

"You mean my father was jealous because he thought I was a happy little kid and he wasn't?"

"Perhaps. I don't know," Barry said.

"You used to tease a lot. Do you still do that?"

"No, I don't do that anymore."

December 9: Danny got separated from Barry at work on the insistence of Mrs. Miller, Danny's mother. Barry is disappointed; he will hardly see Danny anymore. A limb from a eucalyptus tree fell on Barry's trailer roof and frightened him.

"How much pocket money?" Barry asked me.

"How much do you think you will need?"

He wrote down "ten."

"Next week I want to budget out some money to buy Tyler a birthday present. He wants a radio."

"How old will he be?"

"Twenty-eight."

"Oh, he's older than you! I thought you were older because you always talk to him like a father. *He* should play the dad.."

"Could Tyler really be my dad?"

"No, he couldn't. He was only four years old when you were born."

I saw Tyler before me with his fine features, following Barry with his eyes. But unlike his boy friend, Tyler was vivacious and quick. I liked him, but at times his need for attention was so great that with unblinking eyes and non-stop talking he tried to hold me as if with claws. Then I had to shake him off, rudely interrupting his speech in the middle of a sentence.

December 15: Barry and Tyler had to sign a contract not to touch or kiss at work. If they break it, Tyler's privilege to leave his group home to see Barry will be taken away from him.

"It's windy out there," Barry said with concern in his voice.

"Yes, it is. Since I have known you, you have been worrying about falling trees. Usually they don't fall."

"Hm," he said and pointed with his head toward his backyard where he had saved and stacked up the wood from the fallen limb.

"It's good to be in touch with the world out there," he said solemnly and stared out of the window at the waving trees for a long time. Then he resumed writing.

"I guess that's all the bills you have this week," I said. "Here, take my calculator and add everything up."

January 6: Barry asked me where he could get condoms; he and Tyler don't use any. I took him to Thrifty's to show him where they keep them. Danny's sister screamed at Barry to keep away from their house. "Why did she do that, it's none of her business," Barry said to me.

"I think you made an adding mistake," I said. "Let me check it... No, you were right. *I* made the mistake."

"Ho, ho, what's the matter with you," he teased and pushed out a couple of his laughs. "You should go back to high school."

He relished the chance to feel superior.

"Well, I made a mistake. So what? We all make mistakes. But it's true that I'm tired today."

"You must be working too hard. You need a rest," he said with empathy, leaning over and putting his arm around me. It was a gentle but awkward hug. I preferred him to reach out to me psychically. As though he knew, he pulled his arm back at once.

"Here is a bank slip for you to fill out."

January 13: Barry and Tyler got punished for kissing each other at work. Tyler is not allowed to leave his home for three weeks except to go to work. Barry is angry.

January 27: B. has a dislocated shoulder. He was in a fight with his brother.

Barry said, "I'm done. Now what?"

I opened my wallet and dropped the coins and the bills on the table.

"Please count it."

"Oh, now I'm rich. Let's go somewhere. Let's have a date." He loved to make this joke each time we worked on this task.

February 3: Rachel told me today that Barry is going around boasting he has AIDS. She was upset. I informed her that Barry had a blood test and he was HIV negative.

Barry picked up the bills, counted them and put them back on the table.

"Have you talked to your new social worker yet?" I asked Barry.

"No," he said, "Spencer is a knucklehead, I know him, and Rachel isn't any better."

Slowly and painstakingly he counted the coins. Then he counted the bills once more. "Twelve dollars and eighty-six cents."

"Good," I said.

"May I listen to the weather report?"

He turned on the TV. Reagan was on the screen. We heard the last sentences of his speech. Barry said, "If I were President I would give peace to all those people. We don't need any wars."

He waved his arms above his head and shouted, "Hurrah, Barry Haas for President of the United States!" He added in a serious voice, "I would make a good president."

There was a knock at the door. Barry went to open it. I looked out of the window and saw a police car. Barry returned with some papers. It was a complaint about harassment and a restraining order. Mrs. Miller, Danny's mother and conservator, had set it up. The hearing was scheduled for two weeks from now.

Barry was upset. I was angry, and worried about the outcome.

During the next few days I filled out the court papers for Barry while Spencer tried to convince Mrs. Miller to settle the problem with Barry out of court—but with no success.

I felt depressed. I was especially sorry for Danny. Only a year ago his girl friend Susan, the beauty with the auburn hair, with whom he had cuddled up during every lunch break, was transferred from her care home to another facility far away. Because both were handicapped their bond was not considered an issue in the decision to move her. And now Danny was going to lose his friend Barry, too, while his mother thought she was acting in his best interest.

I had met Mrs. Miller once at the bank. Her body seemed hard and insect-like, as though she had pushed warmth and emotions away from her life. I didn't know how to respond to her piercing eyes and self-righteous voice.

Strange to think that Danny, this handsome and gentle person, was her son. When he greeted me in his open and friendly way, he made me feel good. Then he would pull his head in a little and in a flowing movement turn away bashfully. These days I felt that I and my clients were surrounded by a hard, cold world. I slept poorly at night; during the day I didn't want to eat.

Barry, however, was optimistic. "Mrs. Miller will be so shocked when she finds out that Danny loves me." He rubbed his palms together in glee.

Each time I came to see him, he took out his restraining order which by now looked mangled and dirty, and moved his index finger slowly along the lines and mumbled once more the words to me.

"They call me a 'retard' and a homosexual! It makes me so mad."

"These are just different words." I explained, "Once you said to me, 'I know that I'm handicapped but I'm still a good person.'"

He nodded. "It's true."

"And once you told me that you had sex with boys and with girls when you were quite young, and you always knew that it was O.K..? Remember?"

"Yeah, I remember."

A few days later I was sitting at my desk wondering why I was so depressed. Why did I identify with Barry so much? Could it be that I had known a similar experience in my life?

I was examining itchy mosquito bites on my arm, rubbing them gently. I never scratched myself like other people did; I guess I was never allowed to do that as a child. There must have been other rules I was not aware of anymore. It occurred to me suddenly I must be surrounded by dozens of invisible signs. I put myself into a neat little prison! I did it, not the world. I would help Barry as much as I could, but he was acting out his own life story which had little in common with mine. I felt a surge of power. That night I slept deeply: I had begun to separate things out in my mind.

The next day I ordered a cup of tea at a coffee shop. There were candy bars displayed on the counter. I took one without paying for it, sat at the table, unwrapped it, and ate it slowly in plain view. I said to myself, this is the first time that I have shoplifted, and probably the last, and this candy bar tastes delicious. I have broken through a taboo and have come out alive on the other side. Good.

I had to take some documents to the courthouse. On one of them Barry's signature was missing. Should I drive all the way to his home and have him sign it? The door to the judge's chambers was open, and when the secretary disappeared in there, I grasped my pen tightly the way Barry did and signed his name. It almost looked like his writing.

"Oh, good! You have all the signatures," the secretary said to me when she came back. "Then let me take these papers to the judge so that he can sign them."

He did and I strode off smiling.

I thought about the approaching court hearing much of the time. Kim passed through my living room; she was picking up my housemate. She used to be Barry's teacher and knew him well.

"They singled him out because he is gay. The heterosexual couples can hug and kiss and nobody says anything. But Barry has big problems, too," she added while both women moved toward the sliding door. I followed them.

"What problems, tell me!"

"He just doesn't know his boundaries, and his nervous laugh, his teasing..." She opened the door a few inches more. It shrieked.

"I heard his family life is unhealthy," Kim said. They stepped out on the porch. "I'll talk to you..." Her last word was caught between the jamb and the door which closed with a moan and a thud.

I was alone. I had to deal with all this by myself. I didn't like what Kim had said. "Unhealthy relationships," I mused. Being affectionate with his mother—as Barry is—is this unhealthy? I had talked to her on the phone a few times. She spoke hesitatingly with long gaps as though she had to wrestle every word out from a marsh of feelings.

I remembered once I saw her standing on the sidewalk with a friend. I had driven Barry home, and he went over to the two women and put his arm around his mother, stooped and for a moment leaned his head against hers. When they separated, I could see her face overflow with emotion. It seemed she didn't see Barry but rather an ancient god who had descended and singled her out. The expression of adoration and of embarrassment shifted quickly back and forth on her face.

Then Barry came toward me, said good-bye once more through the car window, this time in an almost ceremonial way, and followed the two women to the house. I watched him walk up the driveway with a heavy step, slightly stooped and inspired with a feeling of importance yet with the burden of responsibility also.

What about his father? I wondered. I remembered a silent man, small in comparison to his son. They were loading Barry's furniture onto a truck. There seemed to be no vibration coming from that slight body and even when he was standing close by I easily forgot his presence.

He was supposed to control his son and clearly couldn't. The mother was supposed to separate herself from her son and be on her husband's side, but she wouldn't. And Barry's role was to like girls whereas he preferred boys. None of the family played the game according to the rules. No wonder they were called unhealthy. The thought that the whole family disregarded social expectations put me in a good mood.

Finally the day of the hearing arrived. I knew Barry would be in the courthouse half an hour early. He would sit on one of the benches in the hall and wait for me and say, "I'm so glad you are here. I'm so scared." He would throw his protective shell around me and we would sit there comfortably, feeling close and friendly.

But at 9:30 a.m. Barry hadn't appeared yet. At last I saw him coming up the courthouse steps. There was an air of arrogance around him. He hadn't changed his clothes as I had asked him to the day before but came in his work jeans and a torn T-shirt. At least, instead of his worn-out boots he had put on his new tennis shoes. I felt like reproaching him but didn't. There was no spark in his eyes. His body seemed crusted over with fear and pain and anger. He barely greeted me.

We went inside the courtroom. Mrs. Miller, Danny, his sister and Rachel were sitting together in the last row. We settled in one of the front rows.

I watched the judge and an attorney deal with another case. I noticed that the lawyer talked with his hands, directing invisible people around on a stage only *he* saw while the judge put his hands against his forehead, sometimes over his mouth as though he had to check out the truth of the words against the solid reality of his own body.

Suddenly I noticed that I had forgotten to change my shoes. Here I was in my nice clothes but wearing my old Birkenstocks. Especially the right one looked bad. Once when cooking, egg white had dripped on the instep and had run down to the sole in two dark strands. Now I was glad I hadn't criticized Barry for not dressing up.

He put his elbow on the armrest that separated our seats and without paying attention, he pushed my arm off. A moment later he sprawled on his seat and his right leg pushed against my left one. He seemed oblivious to the fact that it belonged to a human being. I moved my leg away. I felt angry. I felt like kicking Barry. Old feelings of being overlooked, of getting pushed away, invaded me. They are right, I thought, limits have to be set for Barry. I'm too soft with him. This hearing serves him right. A part of me slipped out of my body, moved away from him and settled closer to Mrs. Miller's group.

I remembered an incident at Gerald's house. Barry was leaning over his friend, whispering in his ears, while Gerald, holding a glass and a towel in his hands, was cornered near the sink and twisted his body away from Barry and his wooing.

Spencer, Barry's new social worker, who was sitting behind us, asked Barry softly,

"Do you remember which parts of your order you will accept and which one you want to contest?"

"I can't remember anything," Barry said. "I'll just go along with whatever they say."

Spencer looked surprised and sat back. I was disappointed. Had I hoped Barry would defend in public his love for Danny, that he would shine and make me feel proud of him?

At last it was our turn. The hearing was over in less than five minutes. The judge put a restraining order on both Barry and Danny and decided they couldn't come closer to each other than 25 feet. He impressed on them to stick to that order that would be in effect for three years. They nodded and said "yes."

Out in the hall Spencer said to Barry,

"Look, 25 feet is from this door to that bench over there. If you get any closer to Danny the police can handcuff you and lead you to jail. Jail is a horrible place to be."

I wondered why Spencer had to repeat that threat. Didn't he see that Barry was hurt to the bone and that his voice was so hollow it almost broke? I overheard Mrs. Miller reiterate that Barry followed Danny home so many times, but Rachel to whom she spoke, refused to pay attention.

I looked at the space Spencer had indicated. There was this ugly hole with its 25 feet diameter which now separated two human beings.

When I looked up, everyone had disappeared. It was as if we had attended a burial and were eager to leave.

I thought Barry and Gerald would make a good pair of friends and complement each other: Barry, friendly and outgoing, Gerald fearful and a loner but with a much better mind than Barry.

After a group meeting in his house, Gerald whispered something in my ear. Finally I could make out that he wanted me to take Barry along with me when I was leaving. I understood that he didn't want to be left alone with him, because he didn't know how to protect himself from Barry's sexual advances.

I knew Gerald had other desires. He had daydreams of female partners like the pin-up girls in his bedroom while in reality he was too shy even to look a girl in the face.

Gerald

I KNOCKED AT GERALD'S DOOR. For a long time there was no answer. At last he opened it and said, "Hi," in his deep fuzzy voice. He just stood there. I took a step forward and he finally moved backward to let me in. We both circled the armchair that stood right behind the entrance door.

He went to the wall heater and positioned himself against it so that he could warm his back. His sleek, black cat jumped on top of the VCR that was nearby and made herself comfortable. I sat down at the dining room table

"Are you ready to start cooking?" I asked.

Blond curls surrounded a soft face. His body was not at rest. Ever so often there were tiny movements flowing here and there. After a while he replied, speaking slowly, "I have to go to the store first and buy cheese."

"Why didn't you go before? You had all day."

Many seconds passed. Then he said,

"I went to the post office to buy stamps."

"Why didn't you do everything sooner?"

He didn't answer. He had probably watched TV until the early morning hours, then slept until one o'clock. There wasn't much else he wanted to do. The agency had moved his only friend to another town, and since then Gerald's life had become even more monotonous. But instead of nagging and punishing him, as I had done for the last three years, I had begun to learn from him and to experience time the way he did.

How long was he going to stand there? I waited. But after a while I heard myself saying, "So, are you going now?" He was still standing there, warming his back. Into the silence that was around him he spun his images. Their lines, like threads, crisscrossed the room. They were hanging around his head, dissecting and screening his view, blurring reality.

Suddenly, he made a decisive move, walked to his bedroom, came back with jacket and hat, and left without a word.

My eyes caught two Chinese scrolls that decorated his wall. One showed a ferocious tiger stalking through the jungle while on the other one there was a frightened lady. If you hang the tiger to the right of the woman it would seem the animal was going to attack her any moment, but Gerald had arranged them the other way so that the woman was safe.

A roll of Christmas ribbon stood on the corner of his desk. It was March and it would be there until December. It was at the utmost edge and once in a while it would fall off and he would pick it up and put it back at the same place. I had asked him, "How about storing that ribbon in the closet?"

"I'll need it again at Christmas."

"Christmas is still far away."

"Is it really?" he had asked incredulously.

It was not that he didn't know his dates. He was good at arithmetic, and when adding his budget without a calculator he had only made one mistake during the years I had been working with him.

It seemed as if he didn't experience time in a linear fashion where one event comes after the next one. The events of his life appeared closely grouped together like the items on his desk, where the ribbon and the old TV guides, the shaving lotion and the cassettes and everything else were touching each other and were present simultaneously.

I reached for a National Geographic that lay open displaying pictures of boats of ancient Egypt. I read for a while, then put it down. I discovered a small book on the table. It was a journal Gerald's mother had kept during the few months she was ill before she died. He must have found it recently and put it out for me as I had asked him to do. Her handwriting was hard for him to read.

I had never known his mother. Somehow I felt she was still around. It was because Gerald was in touch with her in some mysterious way and reacted to her invisible presence.

I began to read with curiosity. At once I was startled. This was not a spirit who wrote but a strong and alive human being who struggled against death. She wrote,

It's raining today. The rain has never sounded so beautiful to me. I didn't think that I was going to hear it again. I have never appreciated anything so much as the sound of rain at this moment... How I long to live, now that I know the incredible richness of life...

In another passage she wrote,

Gerald is home today. He is so gentle and beautifully unassuming and humble. I like having him around. His sincere nature is uplifting."

The door opened and Gerald came back with a shopping bag and his mail. He opened a letter and read it.

"I got a letter from my car insurance. I have to go to their office to..." He got stuck in his sentence and began again, "I have to go to their office and..." He was breathing heavily. "I have to go to their office and renew..." Whenever he had to meet people, or thought about meeting people, he was flooded with anxiety and words failed him. After two more starts he could finish his sentence and tell me that he had to renew his insurance.

"Will you come with me?"

"I'll see," I replied.

He washed his hands in the kitchen sink for a long time, then dried them over and over, reluctant to let go of a movement that put him at ease.

After a while he began grating a piece of cheese. He was standing against the counter with his legs slightly crossed, rocking his body back and forth; back and forth. What was he experiencing? I went back to my childhood...

I'm sitting on a swing. Back and forth; back and forth. It's like an addiction. I return to that swing so many times. I want to hold on to something. When I fly through the air, the movement erases the ordinary world and lets me re-experience another state of mind. It brings back a dim memory of oneness and of a different space. But the day comes when I'm finished with the swing and am ready to face this world squarely. For Gerald that day never arrives.

The cat jumped on the table and meowed loudly. Gerald smiled and came over. He held her around her narrow chest and lifted her up so that she stood on her hind legs. There were these sharply defined cat eyes with their golden iris and black slits focused intensely on those big, blurred human eyes. Motionlessly they stared at each other and it seemed their glances were sliding into each other and intermingling while I was totally left out.

He let the cat down and she began her loud meowing again. Gerald looked at me shyly. There was pride in his smile as though the cat were his child and he was sharing with me her achievement. His face was almost embarrassing in its openness. It seemed without bones and its features so soft and movable that every emotion showed. At times I felt it was an independent organ with a life of its own. But I had found that underneath this softness there was a solid core of self-directedness and integrity.

The cat began to paw the open magazine. Gerald pulled it away from her.

"They found this boat," I said and pointed to the picture. "It has been buried for thousands of years."

"Which one is that?" he asked. I showed it to him. "See, parts of it are rotten and some of the planks are broken." He observed this with interest.

"People believed that after you died you had to cross a river before arriving in another world. They put all kinds of things into a person's grave, things the dead person might need on their journey, even a boat." He gazed into space dreamily. I asked him, "What do you think happens when people die?"

He answered promptly, "They will go somewhere and then they will be born again and they will be another person."

"Would you like me to read a passage from your mother's journal?"

"Yes, please." He came closer.

"She wanted her ashes scattered at the coast." I said. I began to read:

There's a very special place where many high spirits hang out: north of Shell Beach, three miles from where the road turns toward Anoka there is a dirt road on your left going up a hill and back toward the coast. It proceeds for about two miles. There is a magic place up there along the ridge which is parallel to the ocean. One is high above the sea with grassy slopes falling away to the ocean with a backdrop of redwoods and pines. My earthly remains long to rest there. The splendor and majesty of this place speaks for itself and for me.

I looked up at Gerald. His face had shifted. He was completely present and vulnerable like a newborn.

"Did this happen?" I asked. "Did your family fulfill her wish?"

He answered in his deepest voice, "We did it, we went there." His words seemed to emanate from a vault, and inaudible echoes were spreading and embracing more and more space.

I saw a group of people climbing toward a ridge. I heard their footsteps on the dry yellow grass and felt the breeze coming from the ocean. Gerald was lagging behind not seeing anything but pouring himself out into the magical place.

"I wish I had known your mother. We might have become close friends."

He nodded.

"How about preparing your casserole now and when it is in the oven I'll read you some more." After a few seconds he said, "What did you say?"

I had spoken too fast without making sure that he was listening. Often I forgot how little he absorbed when people were talking to him, or to each other in his presence. I said more slowly with pauses, "Listen, Gerald... First you prepare your casserole... When it is done, put it in the oven... While it is baking I'll read you more of your mother's journal."

He worked slowly, quietly. Sometimes he stopped in the middle of what he was doing, took a few steps then stared into space, his head slightly raised. What was he imagining? Perhaps what he sensed were jungles with overgrown paths that led to shady ponds, sleek creatures moving by, roots going down so deep... the jungle, a woman, totally embracing him.

I opened the journal again. I read about the struggle with pain, the search for clarity, the reunion of mind and body.

It feels of late so much that my loved ones, each in their own way, are fulfilling a role in the completion and fulfillment of the lifetime of mine. We are a reflection for each other; a pool of truth. Somehow, we all work into each others' destinies. We give and take just what we need to know from the other.

Gerald came closer. "It's in the oven now."

"All right. I'm going to read you what I think is the most important passage of the journal and the most beautiful one." I read it slowly so even if he didn't grasp all the words he could understand from my voice the mood of the writing.

I keep flashing on a vision that I had several years ago. The feeling was one of such high magnitude that I cannot find the words to do it justice. Have you ever felt pure intuition? An experience of total knowing; and complete certainty? That is the way I felt one day when I knew my consciousness is eternal, that it is never-ending;

that it will always be.

I looked up at Gerald. I wanted him to take a chair and make himself comfortable but I realized that his body anticipating deep emotions was in no position to relax. I went on reading.

I was sitting on a large sand dune at a remote beach. It was pushing late afternoon on a clear fall day. The sun was shimmering on the water in such a magical way that the sun and sky and sea started trading places with each other. There was a cosmic energy dance going on that was absolutely blowing all my senses out of my head. It was like I was seeing everything upside down for a moment then it would right itself again and repeat the sequence and all of it flowing in the most gentle way and all clothed in the most exquisite colors of gold and pink. Time and space as I know it, vanished. I became a total-onement with the universe and the Almighty. The truth of that experience has never diminished. I learned at that moment that we all shall live forever.

Gerald was still standing at my side. Not only his lips but his whole face had parted and he was barely holding back something— his soul maybe—as if it could escape at any moment.

I was aware that the room with all its furniture and things had become thin like a web whose threads couldn't cover up behind them the presence of infinite space and timeless existence.

> It's an evening in October. I'm sitting quietly, listening to the silence around me. The hum of an airplane breaks it, then the voice of a child, calling her pet. My cup is almost empty. I'm inhaling the subtle fragrance of lemon and bark. It's the linden tea in my cup that is waking up vague feelings and memories of the old country. I take the last sip and finish it.
>
> The time came when I realized it was right to quit my

job. I felt entangled by the lives of my clients, and my work had become a burden. I needed to be free again and open to new experiences.

Finding a Home

SO MANY THINGS TO TAKE WITH ME! My body is tingling with anticipation. My backpack is almost full and my cooking utensils are not even in yet.

Where are my camping dishes and pots? They must be stored in the shed. So off I go down the dirt path with it's tiny weeds. Manzanita bushes are tapping my arms. It's all so friendly and familiar. I'm rooted here, but not deeply. I don't feel any taproots under my feet in this part of the world. Will I feel them in my home country?

Back to my house. I search the bookshelf and soon find a map of Switzerland. I blow the dust off and stick it in my pack. I'm leaving home to go home.

"Bring your binoculars," I advised my friend Noreen. "We may see marmots or chamois." I'm glad she is coming with me. "And don't forget your little tape machine to record the sounds of cowbells and the alp horn."

What else do I have to pack? " It's awful how much stuff we need in our overly civilized generation," my mother would often say, while closing a rather small suitcase. Have I informed her of the correct date and time of my arrival?

"Dear Mom," I begin my letters and immediately all feelings and emotions fall out of my awareness as through a sieve and all that's left are events: what I did, where I went. Sometimes I write to her about beautiful things I have seen, landscapes or the ocean. I know she likes to hear that. What round-about ways we use to express our affection for each other! I wonder if this could be my last trip to my native country while she is still living? Soon she will be moving to an old age home, her last station.

※

Two months later we were sitting at the Zurich airport. Noreen was at my side, reading. Our vacation was over. It had been a good one and therefore had gone by fast.

I scanned the rows of people who were sitting on armchairs, waiting. I sensed that they didn't want to be there. Almost nobody engaged in conversation as though not wanting to break their transient mood, not wanting to connect.

An incident came back to my mind. Something had struck me as odd when we were in Bangor on our flight east. We had returned to earth at two o'clock in the morning. I stumbled through the waiting room looking at the displays in the gift shops when my eyes caught photographs of country houses for sale. What do they mean by this? I wondered. We just fell out of the sky and will be leaving in half an hour. Why do they offer us a home here? And what is the meaning of all this hectic traveling, this bringing of gifts and buying of souvenirs?

Turning back to Noreen, I said, "I'm relieved that I didn't have to pay overweight for all the luggage I have."

Besides my backpack, I was returning with a suitcase filled with objects from my mother's household. Linen and silverware and other things which she could no longer use. Should I have taken her portrait also, that painting my Vietnamese friend had done many years ago? Though it looked very much like her, there was something unfamiliar about the features, a side of her I didn't know. I saw a strong centrifugal energy in her face as though she were vibrating with faraway forces.

Noreen interrupted my thoughts. "Could you see yourself living in Switzerland again and feeling at home?" she asked.

"I don't know. I was wondering that myself."

I have just arrived in my hometown and am visiting my favorite places. Here it is again, the sober square in front of the unassuming cathedral. I walk over the cobblestones, then gaze down on the Rhine and over to the other shore where the houses with their steep roofs are squeezing each other. The view is infused with a special life. There is still the magic in it I experienced when I was a child.

Still, I'm a little disappointed that I don't feel any pull under my feet; nothing stops me and says "Stay, you are home."

I pass by the mansion where the English Seminar was once housed. I crossed those worn steps so many times as a student. I'm looking up at the window, thinking of Jack, the professor whose support I needed so much then. If he came out of this building now we could talk with each other as equals, joke and laugh together. I imagine it so well, it almost seems it has happened.

"What are you smiling about?" Noreen asked and brought me back to the airport.

"Oh, I don't know…"

A plane was taking off. I looked at my watch once more as if by checking the time I could speed up this waiting period. Then, I was vaguely aware that I didn't really want to leave. The hug my mother had given me this morning was warmer than usual and for a moment her controlled face broke and she had tears in her eyes. I felt she had finally given me permission to love her openly. I gave her another hug and suddenly I realized that I could reach all around her body and take her into my life.

The furniture men stomp up her stairs. They carry away her belongings. She is standing in a corner, leaning on her cane. A few months ago she decided to move because it was the rational thing to do. But now when it is happening, she is in shock and pain.

I accompany her to her new building that smells of paint and plastic. An old woman is sitting on a bench, looking straight ahead without acknowledging us. An employee leads my mother to the dining room. I leave her reluctantly and return to her apartment. I wander through the empty rooms. The wallpaper is worn and, without the curtains the windows look dirty. The rooms look sad. It almost feels as if my mother died. What if that bright, white light that shone into my childhood were extinguished?

Two airline employees, a man and a woman, approached the booth and positioned themselves behind the counter. They exchanged words that made them laugh. Some passengers stepped forward, others lined up behind them. They were handed their boarding cards. An old woman was pushed by in a wheelchair. My mind wandered back to my mother's apartment.

Noreen and I are preparing lunch. The kitchen shelves and drawers are almost bare. Soon everything down to the last spoon will go to the Salvation Army or to the trash. Noreen is looking for a container to mix the salad dressing. She finds a little milk jar and measures the vinegar into it. I feel the taste in my mouth and it puckers. For the last twenty years this jar was only used to put milk in. A tradition is broken. A small death has occurred.

I wondered why this insignificant incident stuck in my mind and why I recalled it now. I remembered an article I had read. A music critic praised a certain concert hall. He thought its excellent acoustics were caused by the fact that only good music was played there, mostly by string orchestras, and so over the years, the molecules of the walls had aligned themselves in such a way as to create the most responsive background for the sounds. It occurred to me that the molecules of our little ceramic jug may also have learned to accommodate the vibrations of the milk in the most harmonious way. Could it be that my mother and I were not overly compulsive when we assigned a specific task to some of our utensils? Were we like the American Indians who knew that their tools have a consciousness of their own and have to be treated with respect?

Another plane was taking off, thundering into the sky.

"They are flying low over our houses on purpose," the old Navajo woman had said. "They want to make us nervous so we will leave our homes. But I'm born here, and here is where I want to be buried. This mountain is sacred, these rivers, this land is sacred."

She had spoken calmly, with dignity. She belonged to a group of reservation women on Big Mountain who addressed a meeting of Whites. Another woman told us of government representatives who had blocked a spring with cement. "The spirits that lived by that spring have left," she added mournfully.

I had wished I could stay with these women.

How rootless I was compared to them! I couldn't even find my father's grave if I cared to. But last week I walked by the house where I grew up. A freeway entrance right behind it cut across the field where I once played. The cherry tree in our yard was gone and so was my apple tree.

I step out of the house. I'm five years old. I'm recovering from an illness and it's the first time I'm allowed to go outdoors into the sunshine. I'm walking over the grass. I feel the urge to bend down, to stretch out my hand and touch the earth. I do it quickly, secretly, so nobody will see me and ask what I am doing. I just know I have to reunite myself with the warm moist ground. An older memory impels me to do so.

I'm much smaller. The trees and the bushes are watching over me, I'm immersed in their rhythm. Is this how it feels being at home? But this was not my oldest memory. There was another one, a more unusual one, one I had forgotten for a long time until one day it emerged with shocking clarity.

More passengers had arrived and almost filled up our section of the lounge.

Noreen looked up from her travel guide. "I didn't know there's so much folklore in the valley where we camped."

I nodded. "I had a friend, a teacher, who grew up in one of the remote valleys. She told me that some of the folks there were still seeing spirits and that there were places where even she would not go after dark." Jokingly I added,"I didn't see any spirits, did you ?"

"Nooo," she said, drawing out her "no." "Spirits are the last thing I want to see." To see spirits I thought I would need the kind of humility that the couple I met in the grove had.

I'm walking through a beach grove. So much light in there, so much space! The sun is showering the bright green leaves with flakes of gold. My steps are inaudible on the soft ground. A couple approaches from the other direction. They are in their late fifties, both portly, conservatively dressed. He is smoking a cigar, she is carrying a handbag.

"Look there, those two!" she cries totally surprised. Both stop. I turn my head. Two crows are sitting on the ground. "Look, they are eating!" There is so much awe and wonderment in her voice that I think I have misunderstood the scene. Perhaps those people are not addressing the crows but maybe pet parrots that have escaped or some other very important beings. I look again. But no, there are only those two crows that are now flying into a tree. The people are still standing and gaping while I continue walking, wondering what they were really seeing.

Days later I'm sitting in a restaurant with Noreen. We wish they would serve us outdoors so that we could look at the splendid white peaks. The waitress seats us at a table with two other women. They tell us that they live in Bern. When one of them gets up, something tiny falls on the table from the folds of her purse. She picks it up and examines it. "You know what it is?" she asks her friend, then answers herself. "It's a piece of onion skin," she smiles. "I went shopping for onions yesterday."

The other woman laughs and, with a knowing expression she says, "You went to the market with your shopping net, and that's how it happened."

An air of complicity is between them. There is as much meaningfulness to their exchange as if they were not talking about an onion skin but perhaps about a little sock from their grandchild.

I reminded Noreen of the incidents with the crows and the onion. We were watching the passengers from the next section of the lounge getting up and lining up in front of their gate. Noreen said, "It seems people here have warm, familial thoughts about onions and things like that."

"Could it be," I asked, "that this country is conservative because the people here feel very much at home with nature ?"

"Maybe," Noreen said and then continued,"I should have read this guide before we were camping in the Alps..."

"No," I interrupted her, "I'm glad you didn't. Imagine how much pressure we would have felt to go here and there and look at this and that."

I recalled how restful it was living without plans and schedules. We had put up our tent under birch trees near a river. Its ice cold water emerged from a glacier high up in the valley.

I'm lying on one of the big boulders that line the shore. It bulges under my body like the back of a friendly being. The granite under my hands and feet is warm and rough. Rocks are wonderful: so solid and reliable. "Grandfather rocks," the Navaho Indian called them. Boulders stick their heads out of the roaring water. The waves wash over them, swirl around them, then reluctantly float downstream with foam on their crests.

I return to our tent and lie down. The rushing sounds envelop me. Behind my closed eyelids the swirling waves are now bright red. I wonder where Noreen is. She must have gone to collect firewood. It feels good to be taken care of.

When I wake up, a fire is crackling. I crawl out of the tent to watch it. The flames dance and shift into a hundred poses. I feel a gentle pull on me as though nature wanted to make friends with me. I'm almost at home in this campground. But not quite.

While we are sitting by the fire an old man approaches. He is wearing a tie and a brown double breasted suit. He might have bought it in the fifties. He is carrying a briefcase that has become malleable with age. He is the camp owner and wants to know if we are all right. He shakes my hand, and immediately he talks about death as though this were the most natural topic to share with a stranger. He is grieving because he feels he has to leave this earth soon. He looks at me questioningly a few times, expecting a response. But what can I say? He beckons me to follow him. Behind a rock he points to a flower. It is a turk's cap lily. I have seen its leaves in several places before, but this is the only one in bloom. I love the sensuous curves of its blossoms. The old man shakes my hand warmly and says he won't be around anymore next time I camp here. I watch him walk across the meadow. I have the feeling he is walking away from his grave.

Noreen closed her book. "We will be boarding in just a few minutes."

What should I have said to the old man? I wondered. Should I have told him my very first memory? That strange vision?

I'm in another existence. There is more light and of a different kind than on earth. A decision has been made, and agreed to by me. I will live on earth for a brief interlude. I go through an immense slowing process until I phase into earth time and arrive here. For a short while I remember where I came from, then I forget. Fifty years later the memory bursts into my mind.

The people in the lounge were getting up. I must have missed the loudspeaker's announcement. We picked up our belongings, lined up at the gate. "San Francisco" was written on the board, "Flight number B86, departure time 10:25."

"In thirteen hours we will be home," Noreen said happily. A temporary home at the most, I thought.